ULSTER ROAD

A Liverpool story of family, love and loss.

By Kathleen Boyle

ULSTER ROAD

ISBN: 9798321301678
© Kathleen Boyle, March, 2023

All rights reserved. No part of this publication may be reproduced,
distributed, or transmitted in any form or by any means,
including photocopying, recording, or other electronic or mechanical methods,
without the prior written permission of the publisher,
except in the case of brief quotations embodied in critical reviews and
certain other non-commercial uses permitted by copyright law.
For permission requests, contact the publisher at the address below.

E-mail: kathdodd2@icloud.com

Cover design: Robin Barratt
Cover image: Canva

Published independently by Robin Barratt
www.RobinBarratt.co.uk

All characters in this book are fictitious and any resemblance to real persons,
either living or dead, is entirely coincidental.

In memory of John

About Kathleen

Kathleen Boyle, née Dodd was born and grew up in Liverpool. She trained as a teacher, then embarked on a career in education spanning five decades in England and worldwide. She has written six novels and a number of illustrated books for children. *Ulster Road* is the third book in her Liverpool series.
E-mail: kathdodd2@icloud.com

~

Other books by Kathleen:

Catherine of Liverpool: A Victorian Workhouse Tale
Parts 1 & 2
ISBN: 978-1731136671

Rosie Jones
ISBN: 979-8534980295

Lotus in the Snow
ISBN: 979-8435196429

The Tale of Craggy Jackson
ISBN: 979-8576911820

The Storyteller of Cotehill Wood
ISBN: 979-8637056422

ULSTER ROAD

Chapter 1

'Mary, luv! Run and tell y'mam y'daddy's home!'

Four year-old Mary tossed the lank fair hair from her eyes and cast a puzzled glance towards Ma Haggerty, the old woman, parked on a rickety wooden chair outside her house and whose shrill voice had bellowed the strange instruction.

It was early spring and Mary clutched two posies of freshly picked daisies which she intended to present to her mother and auntie Jane. She did not remember her father, who went to war in France when she was two years old.

'Run! Quick!' Ma Haggerty shrilled, gazing across the field where once Highfield House stood and was now wild meadowland at the top of Ulster Road in Old Swan.

Mary, her white pinafore grubby with play, scanned the meadow and saw the slender figure of a soldier traipsing through the long grass. A sudden fear rose in her chest and her heart beat faster as she turned and sped home, shouting on the way, 'Mammy! Mammy!'

Sarah Cattell came running to the door of their red brick terraced house.

'Mary! What's up?' she asked, thinking that Mary had a bloodied knee from a fall or a bee sting, situations for which she was always prepared due to having six children to tend.

'Ma Haggerty says I've to tell you Daddy's home.'

Sarah gasped, hands on hips, and wide-eyed with anger.

'Well, Mary, you run and tell Ma Haggerty that's not funny! Not funny at all. Your daddy's a soldier in France,' she faltered, her eyes brim full of tears, then gathering her composure, took a deep breath and bellowed, 'How can he be home? What a cruel thing to say!' She waved her fist toward the hapless neighbour.

'It's true, Mammy.' Said Mary, tugging at her mother's floral pinafore. 'I saw him.' Sarah's teary eyes met her daughter's frightened glare, and she took her by the hand.

'C'mon then, show me.'

As they left the house, the figure of a man in uniform, his eyes the same pale grey as his daughter's blocked their way.

'Alf!' she cried, releasing Mary's hand and grasping her husband's shoulders. 'In the name of all that's holy! Is it you?'

Alfie's shoulders, never what you might call broad and strapping, were bony and his gentle face pale and wizened.

'Aye, it's me, Sarah. Demobbed with bronchitis.' Alfie said, his voice weakened through sickness. He was not an old man, but Sarah saw he had aged beyond his thirty-nine years, since his call up in 1917, when it was made compulsory for fit married men to answer the call. He slipped his hands around her waist and held her close. She smelled of dough and babies, and his heart almost burst with joy. Gone was the scent of death and the misery he had left behind, and here he stood with his wife while little Mary, clutching daisies, looked on, shy and bewildered.

'Put the kettle on the hob, Janie!' Sarah called to her sister. 'My Alfie's home!'

Jane dropped the pile of sheets she was bundling into the dolly tub at the back of the house and rushed to greet her brother-in-law.

'Alfie Cattell, Merciful God! Is this a dream?' She pinched her arm to check. 'Real enough, so it is. Come in and I'll make the tea,'

Alfie took Mary by the hand and gently led her inside to his old chair beside the stove. He picked up his daughter and sat her on his lap.

'I see you've been picking daisies,' he smiled, sweeping the hair from her eyes.

'They're for Mammy and Auntie Jane,' Mary informed him, 'but you can have some.' She pulled a few drooping daisies from a fist-full and gave them to her father.

'Thank you,' he whispered, unable to find the strength to speak. Sarah settled in her chair opposite Alfie and Jane poured the tea.

The room was small and cosy with a brown leather sofa and two armchairs arranged around a blackened, well-scrubbed fire place. There was a polished brass coal scuttle, brush and tongs for adding coal and sweeping the dust. Above the stove were two ornamental brass plates embossed with sailing ships and seagulls, which the couple bought when they married because they reminded Alfie of the days he dreamed about the Pier Head when he was a child in the workhouse. They spoke to him of freedom. Sarah kept the brass-ware shiny bright through polishing, a job now undertaken by seven year-old Eva, their first daughter.

The house from outside was deceptively small, being flanked by two identical houses on either side, and only twenty feet wide, but as with many terraced houses of the day, it stretched a long way back. The kitchen with a long pine table and eight sturdy chairs was located beyond the sitting room, where they were gathered. There was a stove used for baking and stewing. Beyond the kitchen stood the wash room where Jane spent most of her time of late, having given up her job as a live-in maid, to help Sarah with the children when Alf went to France. She now took in washing for the local women, many of whom took the jobs of the men away at war.

Beyond the washroom was a small porch which gave space for shoes and coats. There was a paved yard with a brick construction which housed the toilet, the mangle and dolly tub and, hanging from a nail in the wall, a tin bathtub.

Upstairs were two bedrooms, one for the children with a curtain down the middle to separate the boys from the girls, and two beds in each compartment. The other bedroom was Sarah and Alfie's, but Jane had shared the room with her sister during Alfie's absence. Everything was neat and spotlessly clean.

Mary slid from her father's knee and joined her mother, still shy of the man who had disrupted her afternoon play. There was silence while they drank their tea, each absorbing their shock at the turn of events.

Until yesterday, Alfie had been lying in a hospital bed in Paris, uncertain of his future, after being stretchered there on the brink of death a week earlier. To his surprise, the doctor who was doing the rounds of row upon row of such beds discharged him and he was demobilised.

Sarah and Jane developed a routine of work around the house and caring for the children, unsure when or if they would see Alfie again. There were many tragic reports of soldiers who would never return.

A cry from the kitchen brought their thoughts to the present, and Sarah sprang from her seat and ran through with Mary hot on her heels. She returned with baby Margaret; the child born soon after Alfie left for France, now two years-old and toddling around the house with Mary to catch her if she stumbled. Alfie gazed at the beautiful child whose dark curls fell on plump rosy cheeks and her large brown eyes met his.

'Hello, Margaret,' whispered Alfie, instantly besotted. 'What a beauty!'

They spent a while longer in the front room until Sarah, seeing her husband was visibly exhausted, ordered him to bed.

'You need rest, my love,' said Sarah, placing Margaret on the mat and, taking his hand, helped him out of the chair.

'The children will be home from school soon and you'll need some energy for them,' added Jane.

Alfie willingly consented to being ordered around on this occasion and took himself off to his much dreamed of bed.

Chapter 2

At half past four, the children returned from school. Mary met them at the corner of the alley connecting Ulster Road to Broadgreen Road, a short walk from school.

'Daddy's home,' she shouted, as her brothers approached, racing as usual. Thirteen year-old Alfie, the frontrunner, stopped in his tracks.

'What did y' say, Mary?' he gasped, breathless from running.

'I said Daddy's home, and Mam says you have to be quiet because he's asleep.'

By now eleven year-old Billy and John, eight, had caught up, and the three stood speechless, their dark looks in contrast to Mary's fair pallor, as their little sister delivered the big news.

'He came home across the field and put me on his knee. Now he's asleep.' There was no reason to disbelieve Mary, she was too young to make up such a story. Mary looked beyond them up the back entry to see if Eva, her nine year-old sister, was coming. She would get them organised.

'Where's Eva?' she asked.

'On her way,' Alf answered.

And sure enough, Eva was up in the alley, strolling home with her best friend, Helen. They waited for her, and when Mary told her the news, she whooped with joy, while Alfie shushed her.

'Mam said be quiet, he's asleep,'

Eva calmed and, taking Mary by the hand, whispered a quiet good-bye to Helen.

Ma Haggerty, watching from her doorstep seat smiled as she saw the children step quietly as they approached their house, like a wise old owl, she watched all the goings on of the road, and knew the distress it caused the family when Alf senior was called up to be a soldier in a war, which had already taken the lives of many of the young men in the neighbourhood. But it was hard to believe they would take a man in his late thirties with five children, and one on the way. What a sad world they lived in.

Sarah opened the door of number 37, beaming with excitement, and ushered her children inside.

'Go through to the back room and don't make a sound. Y'dad's home and he needs his sleep,' she whispered, elated to have her family back together under the same roof. Jane placed a plate of home-made bread and butter on the table, and the children helped themselves as they listened to the story of how their father came home, and how Sarah accused poor Ma Haggerty of lying.

'I'll have to say sorry for that,' she sighed. Maggie tugged at her apron and she picked her up to cuddle.

'How is Daddy?' young Alfie asked anxiously. 'Is he alright, not wounded, like?'

Since his father went away, he had grown, not only in stature - a strong boy with a mop of black hair and striking blue eyes - but had assumed responsibility for his siblings, making sure they gave their mother and the new baby some peace and earning a few pennies here and there.

'He's withered and frail, but nothin' we can't fix with time and good food,' Jane informed them, and there was a collective sigh of relief. They had seen the condition of too many young men when they returned without limbs and terribly scarred. A creek from the floor above told them Alfie was awake.

There was tension in the back room as they waited for the man they thought might never return to appear, and when he did, all their worries dissipated with one excited cheer and the children ran to greet him. Alfie hugged the group for a long while, tears in his eyes, until Sarah demanded an end.

'Come on, you lot, let y'Dad breathe,' she said, laughing. 'He's a bit fragile and we'll have to build him up.'

Alfie ruffled the hair of each of his children, then lifted baby Maggie from where she stood beside her mother and planted a great kiss on her cheek.

Looking from one to the other, he sat at the table.

'Come around while I talk to you all,' he said, indicating for the family to join him.

The children he left behind had changed. Young Alf was almost a man, his features chiselled, with the shadow of a moustache appearing. Billy, once skinny and sickly with consumption, had grown strong and healthy under the watchful eye of Sarah and Jane. It was for him they made the move from the city to Ulster Road so that the fresh air would help him heal. Pretty Eva, with her striking blue eyes and dark curls, had the most lovely smile, and held her sister, Mary, close as she waited for him to speak. John had lost his baby features, but he kept his mischievous grin and found it hard to sit still. He was trying his best.

Finally, Maggie, the baby born the week he was posted to France, had now become a toddler with huge brown eyes and a gentle smile.

They gazed at his war-worn face and those with a clear memory of their father before he left were shocked by his appearance. At 41, he appeared old with sunken, sallow cheeks and no twinkle in his eyes.

The stove upon which bubbled a wholesome stew, the like of which Alfie had not enjoyed since he left for war, warmed the room. It was a chilly March day, but in that room the family, complete once again, basked in the warmth of togetherness.

Once all were settled, Alfie delivered the speech he had prepared in his head on the long journey home.

'There were times I never thought this day would come. Times I couldn't see beyond the hour I was dealing with, but you, my family, were never out of my thoughts and it was your faces in my mind's eye that got me through.' He paused for thought, his eyes staring into the distance as if returning to the hellish landscape he left behind. 'Where I've been, and what I've seen, I pray none of you will ever experience, but now we have to be thankful we're together again and I'm in one piece, because, God knows, there are many who aren't or who didn't have the privilege of seeing their loved ones again and we must never forget them.' He bowed his head and the children instinctively followed suit. 'I've dreamed of this day in damp, muddy trenches and in a hospital bed, hot with fever and I honestly thought it would never come, but it has.' He looked each child in the eye and then his wife, Sarah, struggling to hold back her tears. 'It has come, and as a family, we have to make the most of what we've got. It'll take some time for me to get better, and I might be a bit on the quiet side now an' then while I re-adjust, but bear with me. I'll be alright. The worse is over.'

'As long as you don't wallow in it, love,' said Sarah, 'We'll afford you some time, but then you'll have to get back in the race.'

The couple had faced hard and tragic times together in the past and Sarah, too, prepared herself for this moment. She and Alfie witnessed the return of soldiers broken forever. When he was called up, they resolved to try their best to get back on track as soon as possible.

'I know it won't be easy, love, but for the sake of the children, we can't let this blight our lives forever,' she had whispered as they fell asleep the night before he left. 'We must stay strong!'

'Did you see the Eiffel Tower, Daddy?' Asked John.

'Miss Smith, our teacher, said it's very high and in Paris.'

Alfie smiled at his son. 'Yes, lad. I saw the Eiffel Tower and Miss Smith is quite right, it's very high. I'll draw you a picture of it one day.'

'Out and play now all of you, give y'dad some peace for an hour ...' Sarah burst in before a barrage of questions began. Young Alf, you're needed at Pegrams for a few deliveries, Mrs Jones from the shop asked me if you'd be able to call in after school. Eva, take Mary out with you for an hour an' keep an eye on her but have her back here for seven o'clock sharp.'

The children burst into action, fetching footballs and skipping ropes, then dashing outside as if they had been imprisoned for a year, leaving the adults to discuss the serious things in life.

Jane, who had remained quiet throughout the meal, despite the questions she needed to ask, rose from her seat at the table to collect the dishes for washing.

'Have you any news of Callum, Alfie?' she asked nervously, straightening her apron.

'Not a word, Jane.' He answered. 'But there's hope yet; a lot of men waiting to be demobbed. I'd still be there if not for the bronchitis.'

Jane clung to the hope that Callum, her fiancé, would return.

Chapter 3

Pegram's was a grocery shop on the corner of a line of well-established stores in Old Swan, and sold many things for the pantry: sugar, butter, tea, coffee, biscuits, lard, flour, and all the ingredients for any cake imaginable. Young Alf had worked as a delivery boy since his father went to war. Alf senior was the ticket and poster writer for the shop until he got the call up, and Mr Pegram employed his son, part time, as a kind gesture to help the family.

'It's a travesty to take a father of six away from them,' he remarked to Mrs Pegram when he heard the news of Alfie's plight. 'I wouldn't mind if he was the fighting sort, but he's an artist is Alfie. Wouldn't harm a soul. It'll be hard to replace him. His tickets are the best in the Swan.'

'He's gifted,' agreed Betty, busy weighing sugar and pouring it into brown paper packages to line neatly along the dried foods shelf. 'We won't find another like him an' what if he loses his right hand? It's not beyond possible when you look at some of them poor souls at Alder Hey hospital.' There was silence as they pondered the consequences for the family if that came about.

'Anyhow, I'll fix young Alfie up with a spot of delivery; he's a sensible lad.' Mr Pegram concluded.

So, eleven year-old Alfie began his after school rounds, as and when required, cycling the length and breadth of Old Swan with his basket full of goods neatly parcelled and labelled by Mrs Pegram. If he was quick, he might get a tip from some of the generous customers at the end of his round.

Mr Pegram paid him well, and he proudly took the money home for his mother, Sarah, who would take half his earnings - a very welcome addition to their income on top of the soldier's pay and whatever Jane's washing brought in.

Sarah was a confectioner before she married and contributed to their funds by baking to order. Sometimes young Alf would come home from his rounds with news of a soldier's return, and Sarah would bake a cake for him to take to the family. She hoped that the kindness would somehow be repaid in protection for her husband all those miles away.

The day his father returned from the war, Alfie went to work with a spring in his step, feeling the heavy weight of responsibility lift from his whole being. His father was home and now he would be there to hold the baby, soothe Mary, break up the fights and help his mother in all the little ways he had tried to be there for her. Now he could be with his friends whenever he wanted.

The Pegrams were pleased to hear the news.

'I'll have something special for your dad when you finish the round,' said Mr Pegram as he waved Alf off.

It seemed everyone in Old Swan knew Alf senior was home, as his proud son cycled up and down the tightly packed terraces: Belfast Road, Leinster Road, Killarney Road, Donegall Road, then along Broadgreen Road to the big houses in Oakhill Park where trees were plentiful.

'Hiya, Alf, lad! I hear y'dad's home! Tell him welcome back!' came the greetings as he cycled by, feeling happy for the first time in a long time.

Chapter 4

Many of the Ulster Road residents were Irish and, like old Ma Haggerty, had escaped the famine and bore witness to what happened during those terrible times in their old country. Others were descendants of famine victims; fragments of families who took refuge in Liverpool seeking work and a better future and swelled the population so much that the city struggled to provide for the mass of souls seeking shelter and safety. Sarah and Alfie Cattell were among the latter.

They met, fell in love, and started their family whilst living in the city. Both lost loved ones through the White Death, tuberculosis. Alfie's mother died of the disease when he was a child, a tragedy that tore his family apart.

Sarah witnessed the death of two of her sisters, Annie and Emily. Hence, when their second son, Billy was diagnosed with the disease, they moved away from the city smoke, to Ulster Road in Old Swan, where the air was clean.

Old Swan, with its newly built roads grew from a small rural stage coach stop to a thriving community far enough from the city to escape the smoke and close enough for a daily commute to work by tram, bike, horse and cart, or foot; whichever way the traveller chose.

St. Oswald's church, with its graceful spire and grand Gothic interior, provided for the growing Roman Catholic community. It housed a convent with six teaching nuns, two school buildings of grand Victorian style, and a priest's house.

Father Mac, an elderly priest from Dublin, was the leader of the congregation and witnessed the steady rise in the Catholic community numbers. The demands of the parish kept him and Father Pat - a young, energetic, newly ordained priest from Donegal - busy and they were frequent visitors around the houses.

When Father Mac heard Alfie senior was home from the war, he made a few enquiries, and set off to visit the house. He knew the family well and remembered when they first arrived in Old Swan.

They were city dwellers, new to the country life, unused to fields and trees, like almost all the families that joined their community. Some were ragged and barefoot, while others were a little better off, but none could be considered well heeled.

Young Billy was quite sick with consumption back then, but you'd never guess if you saw him now. He could keep up with the other lads, no problem. The older boys and girls went to the school, and all were robust healthy children and well mannered.

'I'm calling on the Cattell's today,' he informed Father Pat at breakfast. 'I hear Alfie's home from the war and think I might be able to help him back to work. I'll find out the lay of the land and see if he's fit enough yet. Seems he had the bronchitis.'

'Lovely family and sure, it's a great thing he came home in one piece, Father.'

'Ay, it is,' agreed Father Mac and, drinking the final dregs of tea, heaved his ageing body from the chair.

'I'll be back to do the Benediction and six o'clock Mass, so need to get along now. These days, my old bones can't handle all the running around.'

'Away with you, Father! You're doin' just fine. There's many a man your age would kill for the energy you have.'

Father Pat smiled. He was fond of 'the boss', as he would often call him. They left the breakfast table to go their separate ways. Father Pat was on the early Mass shift, popular with the workers who wanted to start their day with Holy Communion.

True to his word, Alfie never dwelt on his war years, preferring to pick up where he left off. He was responsible for raising his family, and must set about the task. In his dreams he would return to the field in France where he witnessed unimaginable horror and despair, waking in a fit of terror to find Sarah watching over him, his angel, rough and ready no nonsense Sarah, her dark eyes filled with love and concern. She would enfold him in her arms until he drifted back to sleep.

They never spoke about those dreams; To return with bad dreams was better than not to return at all.

It was a pleasant spring morning when Father Mac called in. Sarah was baking in the kitchen, Jane up to her elbows in Sunlight Soap bubbles as she worked through that day's pile of washing, and Alfie, in the front room keeping watch over Mary and toddler Maggie while smoking his pipe and contemplating the day ahead.

'There y'are Alfie,' said Father Mac when Alfie opened the door and bade him enter. The room looked much smaller once Father Mac stepped inside. His tall, rotund stature almost filled the doorway, much to the alarm of the children who stared in awe at the immense man in a long, black robe.

'Father Mac! Good to see you. Come in and welcome, Mary, tell y'mammy to come through.' Mary took Maggie's hand, unwilling to leave her in the room with the giant, and ran to fetch Sarah.

'Take a seat, father, can I get you a cup of tea?' Sarah asked from the doorway, her hands gooey with the dough she had been kneading when her daughters beckoned.

'To be sure, Sarah, that's good of you, I'd love a brew but can't stay long enough. I'm here for a wee word with your good husband.' He settled himself into an armchair and signed for Alfie - a little startled by the unexpected presence of the priest in his living room - to take a seat.

'I'll get back to me bakin' in that case,' said Sarah, ushering the children into the kitchen and discretely closing the door on the two men.

'Tell me, Alfie, are you settling in? How have you been? I know it's hard, and I'm not going to make y'dwell on the war if y'don't want to, but remember, father Pat and I are around if there's anything y'need to talk about. We've had many a one return to the parish half the man they were before they went, and I'm not saying that would be you, but remember we're here for you.'

He fell silent and studied the face of gentle Alfie, a man not made for fighting, and perceived in his gaunt cheeks and hollowed eyes that the past two years had taken their toll physically and mentally. 'I know, Alfie. I know,' he whispered, and Alfie met his gaze with eyes that exposed the hurt, fear and weariness he had endured.

'I've come with a request,' Father Mac continued. 'I know you've a talent for poster writing, and the parish committee would appreciate your help now and then when they have a special occasion to advertise, Christmas Fairs and the like,'

'I'd be more than happy to help, Father,' Alfie responded, brightening at the thought of putting his skills to use again.

'And I've had a word with an old friend of mine who's well in with one of the floor managers at Coopers grocery store on Church Street, in town. He'd like to meet you for a chat with the possibility of work in the shop.'

'Coopers! For the love of God, Father Mac! That's the best thing I've heard in a long time. I'm willing to help the parish committee one hundred percent, and if I get work at Coopers, I'll be eternally grateful to you, Father. Eternally!'

Father Mac heaved himself out of the chair.

'The least I can do, believe me,' he smiled and, giving his blessing, went on his way, elated to have seen the joy on Alfie's face when he delivered the news; many men were returning from the conflict with no job to go to. In the city, there was unrest and riots between the races, white against black in the pursuit of work and security. With his calligraphy skills, Alfie did not need to worry about finding labour, and anyway, in his weakened state of health, physical work would be beyond him. Coopers was a prestigious up-market shop, and would provide him with a good income to feed his family. Father Mac felt content with his day's work, but there was so much more to do, he thought as he made his way along Ulster Road, where wives chatted on doorsteps and children played.

'Morning, Father!' came the greetings as he strode by.

Chapter 5

'Has to be said, Alf, he came up trumps this time did Father Mac', declared Sarah when the priest was well out of hearing distance. 'I know I've used harsh words about the man in the past, but I can't fault 'im on this one.' She was peeling potatoes with the speed of a machine and dropping them into a huge pan of water. They would later be mashed and accompanied at the table by a full rack of lamb and cabbage to celebrate her husband's return.

'Always said he's a good man,' Alfie responded, watching his wife at work. She spent every day in perpetual motion: cleaning, cooking, shopping, wiping noses, plaiting hair, and seldom stopping until the last child was in bed, when she would put her feet up and have a few laughs about the day. He had missed her to an unbearable degree.

'You're too reverent,' she laughed. 'Anyway, from now on, I won't have a bad thing to say about him, even if he never ever picks one of our lads for the altar.'

Alfie rolled his eyes. 'Not that old chestnut,' he frowned playfully. 'As if any of our lads belonged on the altar. They couldn't be still that long. And besides which, they're not holy enough.'

Sarah threw a potato at him and Alfie, ready for the attack, responded in a flash and caught it.

'Not holy, aren't they? Well, they get that from you, you unholy specimen of a heathen!' she broke into a fit of giggles when Alfie feigned shock and hurt.

'I'll remind you, young lady. I was a choirboy in my day. Stored up enough holiness to last a lifetime, so don't tell me I'm unholy.' He aimed at the pan and threw the potato so it plopped in the water, then ducked into the front room to avoid any further missiles Sarah might fire his way.

Sarah smiled as she peeled away, grateful to have her family complete again. It was good to see her Alfie laugh; there were times she thought she may never see him again and but for her Jane, she couldn't have managed - although it must be said the children pulled their weight. Young Alf had been so strong, bringing in the money and keeping Billy and that little mischief, John in check. A real little man he'd been. And Eva, sweet soul, had watched over Mary and Maggie, and done her share of the housework. She was lucky with her family and couldn't complain.

She put the pan of potatoes on the stove and attacked the enormous cabbage she'd bought at Waterworth's the greengrocers. Mrs Waterworth had been chatting about returning soldiers when she got there and congratulated her on Alfie's return.

'Let's hope life gets back to normal soon, eh Mrs Cattell? We've 'ad enough chaos for our lifetime, although it's almost like the war's come back with the soldiers the way things are in town; with the race riots and that poor man chased to 'is death.' She paused while her customers reflected on the sad and worsening situation around the city centre.

'Lovely cabbage 'ere, Mrs Cattell, I'll knock a bit off the price for you to celebrate the safe homecoming.' Sarah graciously accepted the kind offer, and carried the prize home with mixed feelings. Old Swan was safe from the riots, being almost five miles from the city, but soon Alfie might have to go to work in the city. She hoped and prayed they would find a solution soon. Why was life so complicated when all people needed was to get along, have a decent meal every day, and go about their business?

She heard the front door open and Jane directing Mary to carry a bundle of washing to the back room.

'Take it through Mary, that's a good girl and Maggie, love, in y'go!' The two rosy-cheeked children ran through the kitchen, Mary dragging the bundle while Maggie pushed.

'They're a great help, Mammy,' said Jane, laden with a bundle of her own. 'They carried that load all the way along Ulster Road,' she smiled and winked at her sister. The two women were so alike that a stranger would have a hard time finding the difference.

'Well done, girls!' Sarah gushed, as the two perched on wooden stools beside the fire - a pretty duo with red bows in their hair and starched white pinafores trimmed with lace. Jane insisted the children's clothes should be a good advert for her services. It wouldn't do for her nephews and nieces to roam the streets looking like grubby urchins; although it was a challenge especially with the boys who might have been down a coal mine - the state they were in at the end of a day - but she loved them with all her heart and was grateful to Sarah for putting her up after their father died. She watched them grow and shared the worry when Billy fell ill. She and Sarah struggled together through the war years and rallied each other, while their men were away. And now Alfie was home - but no sign of her Callum, and she feared the worst.

Meanwhile, with Alfie's return, the house was full to the hilt, and she did not want to sleep in the laundry room. Her heart ached for Callum. She imagined he would come home, and they would marry and have a place of their own. She was sure it would happen that way, but for the time being she had to get on with whatever day-to-day life demanded of her.

'Something smells good, Sarah, can I help?' she offered, lifting pan lids to peer inside.

'No thanks, everything is under control, ready for the starving hoards. And speak of the devils ... here they come!' The door flew open, and the house filled with fresh faces excited by the aroma of food that greeted them.

The home-coming meal was the best they had had in a long time: bean soup, succulent lamb, potatoes, cabbage, carrots, and treacle pudding.

Alfie gave a speech before they tucked in, giving thanks for his safe return and for Father Mac, who found him a job.

'And for the ones left behind, may they soon come home to their families,' he concluded, glancing in Jane's direction, meriting a faint smile of acknowledgment from her. After a brief silence, Sarah picked up the serving spoon and the feast began.

Ulster Road was home to at least fifty families, many of whom had one or more children who would be out playing on the street when not at school. Under-fives played close to their own doorstep where their parents could monitor them, while older children wandered further up the road to play with friends or gather on the corner near the meadow. The boys played football, and the girls chatted and skipped or played hopscotch - when the weather permitted. In the winter they stayed outside until Peter, the lamplighter arrived to ignite the tall gas lamps dotted along the road, while during the summer months, when school was closed, they played until mothers called them in; their laughter mingling with the cries of stray seagulls and the chugging of trams that passed the road end on the way to the city.

Neighbours brought chairs out to pass the time of day and have a few laughs once the work was done. Alfie senior's brother, Bill, lived on the other side of the cobbled road with his wife, Mary and son James. The two men enjoyed smoking their pipes and reminiscing. Bill served in the Navy during the early years of the war and was demobilised in 1916, not long before his brother was called up.

The summer of Alfie's return was also a celebration of their re-union. Despite a childhood fraught with hardship, the two formed a close bond after the death of their mother and their broken father's disappearance.

'She'd have loved to be here for this,' said Alf, thoughtfully smoking his pipe late one August evening when the children were indoors, and the road quiet with only a few lingering adults chatting on the kerbside, as the sun gave way to moonlight, and the scent of Sarah's potted clematis wafted on the light breeze.

'Who's that, Alf?' asked Bill.

'Our Catherine,' Alfie replied. 'To think of all that's happened since she passed away, Bill: the children, the War, the move from town. Who'd have thought it? If only she'd have made it, eh? If only we could all be together again, down at the Pier 'ead.' They fell silent, thinking of how things could have been.

'I think she is here, Alfie, lad. We just can't see her.'

'You may be right, Bill, in fact, knowing our Cathy and how she was always looking out for us, it would be odd if she wasn't around,' he laughed.

'How's the job going in the posh shop?' Bill enquired, referring to Coopers where Alf had worked since June - when the doctor pronounced him fit enough. It was a shop that catered for the upper crust of Liverpool society, where porters carried parcels for the shoppers, exotic goods graced the shelves, and the aroma of their famous freshly ground coffee drifted out to Church Street, enticing the moneyed classes to enter, and the poor to dream of what lay beyond the fancy doors.

'Not bad at all. I've my own office and they seem happy enough with what I do; none-stop working, but I don't mind that. I'm doing what I want to do, and it keeps the children in shoes.'

'Father Mac, the hero of the day!' said Bill, happy to know his brother was settled.

'I'll be leaving for America in October, by the way. Got work on a ship sailing on the fourth, and will be away for three months. I was thinking p'raps Jane could move in with us. We've a lot more space, and she could have a room to 'erself while our James sleeps in the little box room. She could still do the laundry at yours.'

Alfie broached the idea with Jane the next day, conscious not to offend her. He knew she was suffering because of Callum's continued absence, and worried she might think she was not welcome to stay where she was close to her sister.

'Are you sure they'll be happy to have me there?' Jane asked. 'I don't want to impose,' she sighed; it was not ideal, but she was weary of sleeping on the makeshift bed in the back room with sheets dangling from washing lines across the ceiling and waking at night to the ghostly shapes they made in the darkness.

'Billy's back on the ships in October and I'm sure Mary will be happy for your company, Janey,' Sarah encouraged. 'And it's just across the road, so we're not far.'

'Makes sense, I suppose,' said Jane. 'I'm sure Callum will come home soon and the two of us will get a place of our own.'

Sarah accidentally dropped the plate she was drying, causing it to smash on the hard tiles. Glad of the distraction from the subject of Callum's return, she busied herself with picking up the pieces.

Chapter 6

Old Swan children loved to watch the blacksmith at work near Blackhorse Lane. Horses were a common sight around Old Swan; pulling carts of farm produce, ploughs and carriages, mingling with motor cars and trams. They were necessary for the smooth running of life; and the blacksmith was a busy man. Young Alf sometimes lent a hand, joined by a few school friends captivated by the volcanic drama of white heat and molten metal which the smithy shaped to the hooves of restless horses, while the young lads soothed and steadied them during the fitting.

Sometimes young Alfie and Billy took off on their bikes to the countryside. Riding through Knotty Ash, past the American soldiers' camp, through Huyton, as far as Lord Derby's estate where lived 'the other half', as Sarah called them.

'Who's the other half, Mammy?' Mary would ask, curious to know more about the mystical half creature.

'All y'need to know, Mary love, is it's nothing like us,'

Sarah would respond unhelpfully, leaving Mary at a loss to imagine the strange being.

Lord Derby's estate was home to the 17th Earl, whose brainchild it was to form the Liverpool Pals Battalions, inspiring thousands of young men to become volunteer soldiers with workmates or neighbours. Young friends filled with pride and honour sent to the Somme together, where many died together.

On one occasion, when August sunshine cast a honey glow across fields of corn, and tree-lined winding roads dappled with leafy shade, the boys reached the estate boundary, marked with high hedges which hid what lay beyond. Although they knew of the manor house, they could never glimpse it and could only imagine its grandeur. They propped their bikes against the hedge and sat on the grass verge to eat homemade jam sandwiches Sarah prepared for them early that day.

'On the way back, we'll pick some blackberries for Mammy,' said Alf leaning against the hedge, swatting a persistent fly from a sunburned leg and enjoying the taste of last year's blackberry crop, preserved in the sandwich. Bill agreed it would be a good idea. He loved the smell of jam bubbling in the huge aluminium pan his mother used every autumn to restock the pantry. Alf was fourteen, and was soon to work full-time on the docks while eleven year-old Bill had a few more years at school.

They lazed in the sunshine, resting from the long ride, drinking cool water from their flasks, and passing the time of day. Alf, startlingly handsome with rugged dark features and piercing blue eyes, was almost a man, and he regarded his little brother with the condescension that often develops between older and younger siblings. Bill had a strong will of his own, and although his brother was bigger and stronger, could hold his own in a fight.

'See the tree at the top of the hill?' Alf said, with a sudden burst of energy. Bill squinted through the sunlight to where the old oak stood alone on the horizon. He sat bolt upright, knowing what would come next. 'Race you there an' back, weaklin'!'

As soon as Alf set off, Bill was on his feet, quickly catching up with his brother as they sped up the hill. Alf reached the tree first, but Bill gathered speed on the downhill stretch and, heart pounding with effort and determination, he jumped on his big brother's back just as he reached their bikes. Alf fell to the ground and the two wrestled in fits of laughter on the warm grass, then drank a little more water.

'Save some for the journey home, Bill,' Alf advised.

They had cycled a few yards towards home, as the sinking sun touched scarlet treetops, when a gunshot shattered the peace of the day, startling Bill so much he lost his balance and toppled onto the gravelly road, hitting his head as he fell. A frightened young boy rushed by carrying a pheasant, while further uphill the angry gunman aimed and fired in their direction.

'What the hell are you doing?' Alf cried, rushing to Bill in a panic. 'Stop with the gun! This is my brother!'

The young thief fled through the fields while an elderly gunman approached unconscious Bill.

'Sorry, lad. I don't aim to hit anyone, but the way it's goin' there'll be no pheasants left an' I'll lose me job. He's in a bad way,' he sighed, lifting Bill in his strong arms. 'Bring the bikes. I'll take you to the house and call the doctor.'

By the time the three reached the gamekeeper's house, Bill was stirring, much to the relief of Alf.

''What happened?' he asked, feeling dazed and wondering why he was laid on a couch, staring at a fancy ceiling.

'Y'fell,' Alf replied. 'Thought you were dead for a while, y'daft beggar.' He smiled at Bill, glad he didn't have to figure out how to tell Mammy.

'What happened and where are we?' Bill asked.

'Mr Giles, the game-keeper, fired his gun, and you went flyin' off your bike. We're in his house while he fetches a doctor.'

'Look at that ceiling, Alf,' said Bill, in awe of the intricate plaster work of leaves and flowers, with now and then a partridge along the cornice.

'If this is the gamekeeper's cottage, how amazing must the big house be?' he muttered, before blacking out again.

When he woke up, he found himself at home with the family anxiously peering down at him. Mr Giles had brought them home in the estate carriage, causing a stir on Ulster Road. The ornate vehicle, pulled by four enormous shire horses, drew up at their house, and the curious neighbours gathered, concerned, as they carried Bill inside. Rumours abounded the child was at death's door, while excited children measured themselves against the giant horses.

'That's the last time you two leave Old Swan!' Sarah scolded.

'Gave me the fright of my life!' Jane put her arm around her sister's shoulders.

'He's going to be alright, Sarah,' she reassured, and Maggie climbed on the bed to stroke her big brother's forehead, while Alf stole quietly away and escaped to the meadow with his football. He'd had enough drama for one day, and a good kick about with friends would get the tension out of his system. He hoped to play for Everton one day, together with most of the lads he knew on Ulster Road, having followed the team to glory in 1915. If his dream was ever to come true, he'd have to practice whenever he got a chance, and now he worked full-time, there would be very few chances. Who would have thought he would find himself on the other side of the hedge at Knowsley Hall, and what a relief to get home to Ulster Road.

Meanwhile, Bill was thinking about the ceiling at the gamekeeper's cottage, and wondering if he might one day create something like that.

Alf senior expressed his gratitude to Mr Giles for fetching the boys home.

'Kind of you, Mr Giles. Some folk would have left them to fend for themselves a fair way from home an' Billy unconscious.'

'Well, I felt responsible, firing the gun an' all. The poachers are a big problem and, like I told young Alf, I'll be sacked if I can't stop them. I never aim to harm, like, just a bit of a scare, but scared the wrong lad today and your poor Bill took the brunt of it.' He rose from his chair. 'I'd better be off then. Need to get the horses back and fed.' He glanced around the room at the children dotted here and there observing the stranger in their midst.

'I'll call in next time I'm passing if that's alright with you, Mr Cattell. Just to see how young Billy's doing.'

'You'll be welcome, Mr Giles, and thanks again.'

Mr Giles became a good friend of the family from that point, and visited them often on his way to town.

Billy recovered well and was fit enough to return to school when term began in September. It was Mary's first year at school and Sarah shed a tear as she saw them off on the day. Bill was in the big boys' school, while Eva and John remained in the infants and Mary would be in the reception class. Eight year-old Eva led her little brother and sister by the hand. She was to take Mary to her classroom before joining her own class. Her best friend, Helen, joined them and took Mary's other hand, offering further encouragement to the nervous child.

'Keep hold of their hands, Eva,' Sarah called from the doorstep as she restrained Maggie, who was eager to join them.

As soon as they were out of view, John broke free and ran ahead, not wanting to be seen holding his sister's hand on the first day back at school. He would never live it down with the other boys in class.

'Come 'ere, y' little tyke!' Eva shouted. 'Mam said you've to stay with us!'

'I'm not holdin' your hand and I won't walk with you!' John responded stubbornly, walking ahead. But he stayed within range of his exasperated sister or else she would yell at him and really show him up. On other occasions, Eva would chase after him and give him a rollicking, but today she had Mary clinging to her hand - just as John had done on his first day.

'You wait till we get home, John!' she scolded. 'I'm telling Mammy!' She turned her attention to Mary.

'When you get there, Mare, there'll be a lot of praying, just put your hands together and close your eyes, then when teacher tells you to sit down, you must sit down an' if she tells you to stand up, stand up, but whatever you do, don't talk,' advised Eva.

'If you talk, she'll whack your hand with a ruler,' Helen added, demonstrating the violent action.

Mary tried to squeeze her hands free so she could make a break for it and run home, but the big girls held tight. There was no escape.

The pink sandstone spire of Saint Oswald's church stood tall against grey clouds as the group joined the throng of other children making their way to the school gate, each with their own thoughts and fears about the day ahead.

'What did you do at school?' asked Sarah when she returned once again in the tight grips of Eva and Helen.

'I said prayers, then I sat down and stood up,' Mary replied, feeling exhausted from the effort of staying quiet and avoiding getting hit with a ruler. She perched on her wooden stool by the stove, pulled bewildered Maggie onto her knee and hugged her tight. Most of the day, her thoughts had been about her little sister. They had spent every day together since Maggie's birth, and Mary ached for her in the high-windowed room on the long wooden bench, her starched pinafore smelling of Auntie Jane's soap, and a huge yellow bow in her fair hair.

'I'm ink and chalk monitor,' Eva proudly announced. She was tired of waiting to be asked - accustomed to being ignored, while one of her more demanding older or younger siblings received lashings of attention.

'You're perfect for the job, Eve,' her mother remarked, smiling at her lovely daughter. Eva was self-sufficient and sensible, with dark curls and eyes as blue as the sky. She was business like as she went about her day

'You're a great help to your mammy, Eve, love. You could get the entire school organised. And I've missed you today.' Eva felt suitably appreciated as she watched her mother roll pastry for the corned beef and onion pie that would grace the table when the family gathered.

Chapter 7

Alfie senior arrived home on the number ten tram at six o'clock every day, Monday to Saturday, and cut a dashing figure in his pinstriped three-piece suit, overcoat and flat cap as he made his way from the tram stop and along Ulster Road. He had nestled into the old routine, as if life had never been interrupted by the trip to France. The city was slowly recovering from the race riots and the police strikes, which had disrupted day-to-day life.

'It's hell in town, Sarah, love. Best stay away for a while,' he advised, grateful to have moved the family away from the city. In the end, it was a good move, and his new job seemed secure.

'You wouldn't believe the money some people have to throw away, Sarah.' he sighed one day as they drank tea together at the kitchen table, enjoying a rare quiet hour while the children played outside, and a September sun sank blanketing the meadow in golden light.

'They come into that shop and spend a hundred pounds or more in an hour and not on anything sensible like a year's supply of food, but frilly things.'

'What do you mean by frilly things?' Sarah laughed, intrigued.

'Night dresses or hats and the men buy silk cravats, as if it matters what you wear in bed or round your neck as long as it keeps y'warm. Imagine wearing fifty pounds round your neck ... or worse still, in bed! We'd feed our family for the best part of a year on that money. I couldn't sleep soundly.'

'Silk's rare, Alf. That's why it costs a lot,' Sarah mused recalling a silk handkerchief her mother brought from Ireland and wondered where it ended up after her death. A precious item lost in time.

'Not as rare as you, my lovely. You're the rarest flower In all the world. I'd much rather have you in my bed than some fancy, silk clad upper-crust type.'

'Glad to know it, husband,' Sarah smiled feigning coyness, and reminding him of the young girl he fell in love with in Sadie Smith's cake shop. Six children and a war later, he was even more in love with her.

'Ahh well, it's not a thing we'll ever have to worry about. When it comes to havin' too much money, we're safe as houses. However, talkin' of money, I'll need to pop to T.J. Hughes' for a few bits and bobs the bairns need now the weather's on the turn, so if you can throw a few shillings my way I'll take the tram to town in the morning.'

'Help y'self from the tin, love,' Alf said, indicating the tobacco tin on the mantelpiece. 'By the way, now that our Alf's working down at the docks, he can contribute to the tin. I'll leave it to you to work out how much.'

It was expected that young workers paid their 'keep' once they started full-time work, and fourteen year-old Alf readily agreed to the amount Sarah requested. He had helped with the family's finances while his father was in France and was happy to contribute his share of the rent.

To celebrate his oldest son's new status in the workforce, Alfie took him to the Swan Inn and bought him his first pint.

As autumn settled in, the boys would collect fallen seeds from beneath horse chestnut trees that lined the streets, then split them, hoping to find a champion conker nestled within. John had a talent for the game, and could beat most of the Ulster Road boys - except one or two he suspected of cheating by hardening them. Whenever he played the cheaters, he used his own 'seasoner' specially treated with boiled vinegar and a brief bake in the oven.

'Our John's at it again, Mam', Eva complained, holding her nose against the acrid stink of vinegar. 'Conkers! They're all over the house; can't move for them!'

It was a Saturday morning and with Alf senior and junior at work, Billy and John playing football on the meadow, and Mary and Maggie out with Jane delivering laundry with the pram doubling as a means of transporting piles of neatly stacked bedding, Sarah and Eva were busy with housework.

Sarah smiled fondly at the thought of John; it was true there were small piles of his conkers dotted around the house wherever he'd emptied his pockets after a gathering spree with his mates. He would return enthused from an after-school expedition around Oakhill Park, where there was always a good supply.

'Beats me how there's a horse chestnut tree left with all the boys plundering their seeds,' she laughed. 'Pop to the larder and fetch a bag of flour, Eva. I'll make a few scones for tea.'

Eva, did as she was bid, standing on a small stool and reaching for a high shelf of the well-stocked larder filled with an abundance of ingredients for baking cakes and pastries, and the lingering aroma of exotic spices.

'Need anythin' else while I'm here, Mam?'

'No, love, I've got the butter and sugar ready,'

Eva watched as her mother measured the dry ingredients into the old yellow mixing bowl which was older than Eva.

'Rub in the butter, while I whisk the eggs,' said Sarah, sliding the bowl across the table to where her daughter stood. Eva knew what to do, having watched the process on countless occasions. She could make scones and simple cakes almost as well as her mother. She lightly rubbed the butter into the flour until the mix looked like bread-crumbs, then Sarah stirred in the eggs and a drop of sour milk to make a soft, sticky dough, then scattering flour on the wooden table, she gently scooped the dough from the bowl, kneaded it and rolled it flat. Eva's favourite part in the process was the cutting to shape the scones. Then she would place them in neat rows on the baking tray, ready for her mother to brush the tops with milk and deliver to the hot oven to bake for fifteen minutes, after which time they would emerge transformed to twice the size and golden brown. She would watch as Sarah transferred twenty hot scones to a cooling tray and smile with the satisfaction of a job well done.

At six o'clock, the family gathered at the table to enjoy plates of scouse, followed by jam and scones.

'You can thank Eva for the scones,' said Sarah 'She's a dab hand at baking now.'

'Almost as good as you, dearest wife,' Alfie smiled and winked at Eva, who blushed a little. 'Your mother was taught by the best,'

'Sadie Smith,' Sarah affirmed.

'I first set eyes on your mammy in Sadie Smith's bakery and it was love at first sight. She appeared from the back of the shop, brandishin' an apple pie. What a beauty! I'll tell y'somethin' my family never ate so many cakes after that. I was in that shop every day until I plucked the courage to ask her out,'

'An what did she say?' John asked, sinking his teeth into a jammy scone.

'What do you think?' Alfie laughed, and the others joined in.

'I married her, so ...'

'Oh, yes!' John interrupted, 'She said a great big yes!'

There was laughter around the table and Sarah reached for her husband's hand.

'And never a moment's regret,' she said. 'Now then, Eva and Mary, take a few scones to Ma Haggerty to have with a cup of tea. Tell her I'll call in with your auntie Jane tomorrow mornin' for a chat.' She put the scones in a basket and covered them with a clean cloth, then saw the two girls out the front door and onto the road where the light was fading, and only a few children gathered in the glow of street lamps.

'Come straight back, girls,' she called as they set off to the end house where Ma Haggerty was wishing her neighbours good night and taking her chair indoors.

'Ma Haggerty,' Eva ventured. The old woman turned her tired face toward the children.

'Are y'after me, girlies?' she asked, peering through the gloom.

'Our mam sent these scones to have with a cup of tea,' Eva said, lifting the basket while Mary gripped the handle with her.

'Is it Sarah's girls?'

'Yes, it is, Ma Haggerty.' Eva confirmed, pushing the basket in her direction. Neither child wanted to linger at the door beyond which lay silence and the weak glow of a lantern.

Ma took the basket. 'Tell y'mam thank you. She's a kind soul, and Lord knows we need more of them in his cruel world, so we do.'

'She said she'll be over for a chat with Auntie Jane in the mornin',' Mary whispered.

'What's that you say?'

'Mam an' Auntie Jane will come for a chat in the mornin',' Eva clarified.

'I'll look forward to it, so I will. God bless you now and hurry home. It's chilly out here.' She watched them run back to their house, lingering a while longer to listen to the swallows gathering in chattering flocks on the rooftops before closing the door on another day.

True to her word, the next morning, Sarah and Jane found an hour in their busy day to go up the road to Ma Haggerty's where they found her already seated outside her house. The road was dappled with autumn leaves, soggy with the fine drizzle that had greeted the day but now gave way to bright sunshine and a few drifting clouds.

'There y'are, lasses!' Ma beamed when she saw the two who had brought along their own chairs to join her. 'Sure, I haven't touched none of those scones yet, thought I'd save them for your visit. I'll fetch them now' Will y'ave a dollop of jam on them?'

'That'll be great, Ma,' said Jane, positioning her chair where she could catch a sunbeam.

'Can I help?' Sarah offered.

'No, lassie, you sit yerself down an' I'll bring a tray, so I will.'

As often happened when two or three gathered, a few more were attracted, and before long, a small group formed, and more tea arrived. There would be the usual gossip and catch up on each other's family news then, Ma Haggerty would sing. The songs she sang were the old style, Irish, Sean Nos, and it was as if the lyrics had emerged from a plot of the Irish soil she was forced to leave when she was ten or else starve to death. She and other old folk living on Ulster Road would never forget the suffering they witnessed, or the love they held for the old country. Sarah and Jane joined in with a few words now and then, learned from their mother, who brought the songs out of Ireland with her and would sometimes sing to them on dark winter evenings beside the stove. And although their mother had passed, they felt her presence when they joined Ma Haggerty for a singing session.

These impromptu gatherings soothed the souls of the women whose lives left little time to relax but each would go back to their day's work uplifted and energised.

'Ma Haggerty's looking frail these days,' Sarah observed when she and Jane returned. 'Best keep an eye on her and make sure she stays warm this winter.'

Chapter 8

The last leaves of autumn were ripped from sturdy trees by winds so strong the children walked to school braving the gusts and holding each other's hands to stay anchored. At school, their spirits were as wild as the wind, and they found it hard to remain still at their desks. When the winds subsided, bright leaves drifted along the cobbles, soon to be replaced by slippery winter frost and days so short they hardly existed. Now muffled in scarves and gloves knitted by Jane, who had settled in her new home with Billy and Mary. Despite the teachers' efforts to warm their classroom by lighting fires in the neglected fireplaces, the children shivered on school benches.

    Sarah fished out last winter's woollen socks to see what could be salvaged with her darning needle. Young Billy, whose chest was weakened by consumption, was a source of worry for her. She was determined the dreadful disease would never again take one of her loved ones and made beef broth and spare rib soup, scouse, and bubble and squeak, apple pies and rice pudding, all cheap, hot meals ready for her family at the end of their busy days.

    Mornings she would send them out with salted porridge - the way her Scottish father used to make it; solid slabs of oats and milk that took a while to digest. Young Alf worked shifts at the docks, and there was always something waiting for him on the stove, whatever time he came home.

    Despite Sarah's best efforts, Eva and John fell ill with fever in December. The influenza - known as Spanish flu - that ravaged the population during the final months of war, remained a threat, as well as typhoid, cholera and scarlet fever, and so when sickness visited, fear ensued. They moved the two to Sarah and Alfie's room, where they could keep an eye on them through the night.

'You're a bundle of nerves, Sarah,' Alfie whispered as they lay in bed one freezing night. A small fire burned in the grate, and the room smelled of smoke and medication. Eva and John's rasping breaths punctuated the stillness.

'And why wouldn't I be? It frightens me to see them this way, Alf. I can't help but think of our Annie and James who died when they'd hardly lived, and your mam and poor Catherine. I look at their sick little faces and can't stop worrying and praying.'

'I can't deny I feel the same, but we have to stay hopeful and do the best we can, love. You sleep a while and I'll stay awake to check on them.'

'Will you Alf? Promise you won't fall asleep. Keep listening to their breaths and if one stops, wake me.'

'I'll do that. Now sleep.' he kissed her neck and held her close. But Sarah couldn't sleep; she lay awake, aware of every change in the rhythm of inhales and exhales of Eva and John.

The family went about their business in near silence while they waited for the fever to pass, but life goes on and there were six healthy mouths to feed and a house to maintain. Mary took over Eva's brass polishing duty with a little help from Maggie.

Young Billy ran errands for Sarah and got himself a job at Pegrams. so impressed was Mr Pegram with Alf's performance, he didn't hesitate when his younger brother Bill enquired about a delivery round.

'I want to be a plasterer,' Billy told his new boss. 'But can't start the apprenticeship 'til I'm fourteen.'

'Good for you, lad,' Mr Pegram said. 'There'll always be a need for plasterers, with all the buildin' goin' on in town. You'll have a job for life!'

'Ay, I'd love to work on them fancy ceilings y' see in big houses. I saw one in the game-keeper's lodge when I fell off me bike.'

'Don't go fallin' off that bike, Billy, lad,' Mr Pegram laughed as he watched him leave laden with paper packages and boxes of goods.

'I'll try not to, Mr Pegram, but have to hurry today. Told me mam I'd be home early with a cabbage and a few spuds. Our Eva an' John are poorly with fever an' she doesn't want to leave them.' Billy waved and sped off around Old Swan as if he had a train to catch within the hour.

'Oh dear!' Mrs Pegram sighed. 'That fever could be any number of things. I wonder if Sarah's had a doctor to see them. There are too many little ones struck down with fever of one sort or another.'

'Not much can be done about it but wait and see,' said Mr Pegram, reaching for the sugar bags to fill a few and restock the shelf. 'I'll put a little box of stuff together for Billy to take home. They're a good family an' that Sarah did a lot for the bereaved when the war was on. Speaking of which, I thought I saw Callum, Jane's sweetheart up The Swan yesterday. He must be back at last.'

'Callum? Well, that's good news,' said Mrs Pegram. 'I thought Jane would never see him again. I'll ask Billy when he returns.'

When Billy arrived home with the parcel of lemons, honey, tea, sugar and milk sent by the Pegrams, as well as the cabbage and potatoes she asked for, Sarah was full of gratitude and set about making a vegetable broth with barley and lentils. She and Jane had taken turns to sit with Eva and John throughout the day.

Sarah swore never to scold John for flinging open the back door and running through the house in his muddy football boots. She bathed his forehead with cold water, sweeping wet strands of fair hair back to cool him. He was such a ball of energy, always active. She hardly ever had a quiet time with him, and Eva was the opposite, a worrier.

'I won't ask so much of her when she's better,' thought Sarah. 'She's always looking after her brothers and sisters. My little blue-eyed angel.'

Two days passed with no change in either child. Father Mac dropped by to give his blessing.

'There's a lot of it about, Mrs Cattell. I've seen many of the parish children in this condition. Most recover,' he said, avoiding eye contact with the anxious mother; for both knew that some did not. Eva's fever broke the next day, and she joined the vigil over John from her own sickbed until his fever left him, and he too began the slow recovery with drinks of hot honeyed lemon and bowls of nourishing winter broth.

The dark cloud shifted from the house and Christmas, all trace of which had been banished while the children were sick, was permitted to enter. Ingredients for the festive cake were mustered together, and Mary and Maggie jumped with excitement as a huge cake tin was retrieved from the top shelf of the pantry. Then the dried fruit, flour, treacle, syrup, brown sugar, eggs, cinnamon, nutmeg and ginger. And then the mixing and finger licking when great globs of fruity mixture filled the tin and the warm spicy aroma wafted through the house while the cake slowly baked.

'Don't open that oven until the cake comes out!' Sarah commanded, reaching for a large jar of mincemeat for the mince pies. 'If y'do it'll sink and be flat as a pancake!'

Alfie senior returned on the tram to find the Christmas decorations had been dusted off and hung, and the house was transformed as his first Christmas at home since returning from war was underway.

The Old Swan shops filled with festive fare, and Carol singers gathered around a bright Christmas tree on the corner of Ulster Road, jovial women muffled in fur-trimmed coats and men sporting top hats evocative of days gone by. Trams packed with Christmas shoppers trundled to and fro, laden with boxes and bags of wares to brighten the season.

Sarah was grateful to have Alfie home while others grieved their loss.

'I thought we might have seen Callum around the house this Christmas, Auntie Jane,' Billy remarked, as he and Jane took a tea break in the kitchen on Christmas Eve. Billy had worked flat out delivering for Pegrams since school broke up, and Jane's laundry work was never ending. His casual tone shocked Jane.

'That's a callous thing to say, Bill. How can you have such a thought when it's fairly obvious Callum won't be around this Christmas or any other?' She raised her voice in a manner seldom heard from Jane, and her nephew cringed with embarrassment.

'Sorry, Auntie Jane, I thought he was home after what Mrs Pegram said the other day.'

'Mrs Pegram? What would she know about my Callum?'

'She said she saw him in Old Swan and I thought he would have been in touch, like.'

Silence ensued while Jane reflected on his words, and Billy sat motionless on the stool beside the fire. An uncomfortable minute ticked by before Jane flung off her apron, donned her coat, and strode out of the house.

Sarah arrived home from shopping with Mary and Maggie in time to bump into her sister on the doorstep, but Jane met her greeting with a horrified glare and ran up Ulster Road towards the shops.

'What's got into Auntie Jane?' asked Sarah, removing her coat, hat and gloves and helping her bright-eyed daughters with the task.

'Bill, move over and let these two near the stove, it's freezin' out there.'

Billy rose from the stool and made way for his little sisters to get closer to the warm glow.

'I only asked her if we'd see Callum over Christmas, Mam.'

Sarah dropped the kettle she was filling with water for a pot of tea. It clattered into the sink.

'You did what?' Sarah exploded, the colour draining from her cheeks.

'Mrs Pegram said she saw him around Old Swan and I only thought I'd ask about him.'

'Dear God, Billy! What on earth were y' thinkin'? Today of all days! Mind you, what's Mrs Pegram on about?' her anger turned to puzzlement and she resumed her tea making task, disappointed that Jane was not around to share a hot drink and catch up on the Old Swan gossip. It would seem Jane and her fiancé, Callum, were now the gossip. But how could he be seen around without Jane knowing? Perhaps he intended to surprise her for Christmas, and now the plan was spoiled. She settled on a wooden chair at the table to ponder briefly and drink the hot tea, warming her hands on the cup.

'Oh, well, it's not your fault, son. It was an innocent question under the circumstances.'

Billy, relieved by this acknowledgement, pulled his jacket on.

'Thanks for that, Mam. I meant nothing by it. Hope Auntie Jane's alright. I've a few more deliveries to do, so see you later!'

'Bye, Billy! Not too late, lad. You'll need to scrub up for tomorrow.'

Alf senior arrived home to find Eva and John on the sofa in the front room, snug beneath blankets and looking livelier than they had for a while. The fever left them lethargic and Sarah had insisted they remain in the main bedroom so she could keep an eye on them. It was good to see them downstairs, albeit not fully ready to venture out into the bitter cold.

'Back with us at last,' Alfie smiled. 'Welcome to the world again!' He pulled two colourful lollipops from his pocket and handed them to the children, who brightened at the sight, whereupon Mary and Maggie came running from the kitchen in the hope their daddy had a few more hidden away, which he did. The two girls joined their brother and sister on the sofa, and all four settled to enjoy their sweet surprise. Alfie delighted at the sight, and his heart leapt with pride to see them together and alive after the scare.

He was weary after a busy month at work, writing the Christmas tickets and posters, a job he enjoyed but in a big shop like Coopers the demand was relentless, and mistakes frowned upon as there were high expectations of quality work to please the 'quality' customers.

True to his word, Alfie also provided the church hall committee with the posters they ordered advertising the Christmas fare, as well as the tickets for their stalls.

The tempting aroma of baking coming from the kitchen beckoned Alfie where he was greeted by Sarah, elbow deep in flour.

'You're a busy bee, my darlin' wife.' He stole a mince pie from the cooling tray and ducked to avoid the handful of flour Sarah flung his way.

'That's your last until tomorrow, me laddo!' she scolded.

'Not bad, though. In fact, every bit as good as Cooper's café.'

'Is that so?' Sarah responded, flattered by the remark. 'I'll allow you one more for those kind words,' she laughed.

'One's enough for now, thanks. Where's our Jane?'

It was unusual for Jane not to be scrubbing or ironing in the scullery.

'Thereby hangs a tale, Alf,'

'What's up?' Alf asked.

Sarah recounted the events of the morning to the point where she was almost sent flying on the doorstep by Jane's hasty exit.

'She hasn't been home since,' She concluded.

Chapter 9

'Mary, love, take this bundle across to Ma Haggerty an' tell her I'll be over later,' Sarah put the bundle of festive goodies in a basket and handed it to little Mary. 'Y'can take Maggie with you but hold her hand tight. What do you have to say to Ma Haggerty?'

'Happy Christmas?' Mary ventured. The responsibility was new to her, always having relied on big sister Eva to do the talking.

'Well, yes, you can say that, but then what?' Mary wracked her brains for something else to say.

'How are you?' she smiled, certain that would be the answer.

'No, Mary, I told you just a minute ago,' Sarah sighed. Mary was the dreamer of her brood. 'I said, tell her I'll be over later!'

'Oh. Yes! You'll be over later. I'll tell her that, C'mon Mag.' She picked up the basket and took Maggie's hand as Sarah opened the door and stood on the step to watch as they crossed the cobbled road and made their way to MaHaggerty's. It was too cold for Ma to be out on her chair, and considering her great age there would not be many more springs she would oversee the goings on along Ulster Road.

Mary tapped the door gently and waited patiently. The two girls wore thick red coats over their pinafores and green berries Sarah had picked up from the bargain basket at T. J Hughes' store in town. Jane had knitted their green scarfs and gloves last winter. There was always a good selection of such items collected over the years.

Ma Haggerty did not come to the door, so Mary gently tapped again and stood ready with her sweet smile for the old lady to appear as she always would when Eva knocked. Maggie was less patient than her big sister, and after a few seconds banged loud and long on the door. Mary cringed and felt her face burn with embarrassment as she noticed various doorstep gossipers, look their way.

'Maggie! It's not polite to bang like that!' she scolded, whereupon Ma Haggerty opened the door. She tried to regain her composure and remember what had to be said.

'Happy Christmas!' she smiled, handing over the basket.

'Well, now, if it isn't Mary an' Maggie Cattell, come to wish an old Irish woman a happy Christmas,' Ma Haggerty grinned a toothless grin. She wore layers of what appeared to be rags, but were in fact woollen shawls of various age and faded colours; green, blue and purple - resembling the Irish landscape of her childhood, and her grey hair was covered by a blue felt bonnet which drew out the bright blue of her eyes.

'Why don't you come in, girls? I've a little somethin' for you. How's your Eva and John?'

Mary panicked, unwilling to enter the house. 'We can't come in Ma, our mammy said we have to go straight home ...' she stammered, her normally pale cheeks blushing almost to match the colour of her coat. 'And John and Eve are gettin' better.'

'Wait there a minute in that case.' They waited for what seemed like a very long time for Ma to return with a shawl knotted to form a sack in which she had placed a few items the girls could not yet glimpse.

'Give this to your mam and tell her to keep the shawl. She placed her bundle in the basket and gave it to Mary, who by now wished she had never been selected for the job and dearly wanted Eva to be back on her feet and able to resume her role. She took Maggie's hand and turned to go, but Maggie pulled her back.

'What you doin' Mag? Let's go!' but the little one stood firm, her big dark eyes looking from Mary to Ma.

'What is it?' Mary asked impatiently, before remembering her mammy's words. She turned to Ma, and pulling herself full height, delivered the message: 'Mam said she'll be over later.'

'Tell her I'll have a bottle of stout waiting for her!' Ma said, closing the door on the cold. Mary was a bit put out to have another message to deliver, having already fulfilled one such obligation. She held tight to Maggie, who had in fact saved the day, as they crossed the road to the safety of home.

Chaos reigned in the house as Sarah juggled with the jobs that needed doing to prepare for the big day. Uncle Billy and Auntie Mary would come from across the road with their son James and a few extra chairs, and Granddad John would also be joining them for dinner. There was no sign of Jane, so Sarah delegated jobs.

'Alf an' Bill, peel the spuds, Eva an' John chop the cabbage and carrots. Y'father's in charge of the pheasant. Mary an' Mag, polish the brasses. I'm havin' a sit down for five minutes with a cup of tea.'

'Mammy, Ma Haggerty said she'll 'ave a bottle of stout ready for you,' said Mary, pulling out the polishing paraphernalia from the cupboard under the stairs, and feeling quite grown up for delivering two important messages in one day.

'I'll not stay there long, mind. So much to do!' Sarah felt excessively tired that day and needed to rest, as unbeknownst to anyone else, she was pregnant again and waiting for the right moment to tell Alfie senior, but the right moment was hard to find in their busy household.

'Eva, we'll 'ave to ask Auntie Mary t'bring some plates over in the mornin''

Eva made a mental note as she chopped the cabbage - her brief recovery time over, although she still felt groggy and her legs ached. John slinked off, having attempted to peel two carrots and returned to the front room sofa by the fire where he could admire the Christmas tree his big brother Alf brought back from the docks where an old lag of a sailor was selling them for tuppence a tree. It had yet to be decorated, but John loved the smell of pine, and the fact there was an actual tree in their house.

Somehow, chaos turned to calm, and the house settled into an edgy anticipation of the day, like a bride before her wedding. Sarah set the bathtub, which had been brought in from the yard, before the fire in the front room and scrubbed her younger children clean. Then she replenished the water for Bill and Alfie to bathe with more privacy. She and Alf senior would bathe once the children were asleep. When the younger ones hung their old socks up for Santa, they went excitedly to bed, whereupon Alf senior and Alf junior set off to the Swan Inn where they had arranged to meet Mr Giles, the gamekeeper, who promised to bring a pheasant for tomorrow's dinner, while Sarah decorated the tree, lamenting that she had not found the time to visit Ma Haggerty.

'That poor woman all alone in her cold house and I haven't had a minute in the day to call in on her.' She need not have worried, as Ma had a small gathering of Ulster Road folk who went to reminisce about the Old Country and its ways, and much later they would trundle in a horse-drawn carriage to Midnight Mass.

At half-past nine, when Sarah was bathed and ready for bed, Jane arrived, her face pale and distressed.

'Jane, love! Sit down and I'll make us a cup of tea,' said Sarah, gently taking her sister by the arm, but Jane withdrew.

'I'll not stay. Just wanted you to know I'm back but can't talk about anything tonight. I'll see you in the morning and sorry I've been as much use as a chocolate teapot today, but will make up for it I promise. There's news, but it's not good.'

'Is Callum alive?' Sarah ventured, hoping for an iota of information.

'He's alive,' Jane turned to the door and, without a backward glance, left the house.

It was too much of a mystery for Sarah to dwell upon, and her head spun after the demands of the day. She added a few lumps of coal to the dwindling fire and eased herself into her chair with thoughts skipping between dinner plans, Jane's troubles and the baby inside her, of which only she was aware. In the morning, she thought, I'll have time to do everything while the children are at Mass with Alfie. Then it occurred to her the children would need to look presentable for church and normally Jane would have their clothes laundered, but nothing was normal now with this Callum business. Had he found someone else? Whatever it was seemed to have upset her sister in a big way. Such a terrible thing to have their wedding plans ruined by that cursed war.

Jane and Callum had been sweethearts since they met in service at one of the big houses in Newsham Park. She was a maid, and he worked in the stables. They waited a few years to get engaged because romance between the workers was forbidden. Sarah recalled the day Jane left her post for good, and brought Callum to their home on Peach Street to announce their engagement. They were a handsome couple with a bright future before the war.

The soft sound of footsteps brought Sarah back to the present where Mary stood on the bottom stair, rubbing her sleepy eyes, angelic, with her tousle of fair hair and pink cheeks.

'Has he been?' she asked.

'Mary! Has who been?'

'Father Christmas,' Mary whispered, afraid she might scare him off if he happened to be on his way down the chimney.

'No, my love, not yet an' he won't come if you're not asleep, so get back to bed an' don't wake the others,' Mary scooted back to bed, and Sarah smiled at her innocence. If only life remained so simple and magical.

She heaved her tired body out of the chair and went to the washroom, which Jane usually kept neat and well organized with labelled bundles of pressed clothes, tableware, sheets, and pillowcases. However, after her sudden departure, it was left in a state. Sarah rummaged among the pile on the shelf where she kept the children's clothes, and pulled out three white pinafores for Maggie, Mary and Eva and white shirts for Alf and the boys. Their dresses and breeches already hung in the bedrooms. After ironing the clothes, she filled six Christmas stockings with nuts, tangerines and a few simple gifts. Ma Haggerty had made the girls peg dolls, and a small pouch of marbles for John. Feeling faint with weariness, she banked up the fire and climbed the stairs to bed.

She was sleeping when the two men returned from a festive Christmas Eve at the pub. Young Alf went straight to bed while his father hung the copper feathered pheasant in the pantry and left a gift on the table for his Sarah before creeping up the stairs to join her in slumber.

Chapter 10

Granddad John set off early on Christmas morning to walk from the town centre to Ulster Road in Old Swan. It was a crisp, frosty morning adorned by a pale blue sky and the streets of Liverpool were quiet.

John was an elderly man and his progress was slow, but he enjoyed the walk along the familiar route. He once lived in a cottage in Knotty Ash and, as he walked, recalled his journeys to and from the cottage before the building of the Irish streets. Old Swan was a rural idyll and Highfield House, an imposing manor, stood proudly beyond its keeper's gates.

There had been many changes since then. It was not a good time for John, who took to drink after the death of his wife Anne Marie, leaving his three children in the care of his sister-in-law Lizzie who, unbeknownst to him, put them in the workhouse.

She wasn't to blame for that, he conceded. They were his responsibility, and had he not returned for them, who knows what would have become of the three? He did his best.

The buildings became sparse as he walked until he reached the edge of the city, with its thick coat of soot, and entered leafier districts beyond reach of the smoke. He thought about Billy and Alfie - his sons - how well they had done for themselves, Billy the sailor, and Alf a sign-writer. He was always an artist, like his dad. John smiled. He thought about his wife, Anne Marie and hoped she'd forgive him for deserting the children. Catherine, his daughter, would be with her now.

A robin landed on the fence to his right and he stopped to admire the bright red of its breast. It flew away, but he lingered a while at the gate. Billy never forgave. No matter what he did or how hard he tried, Billy never forgave, but would tolerate him on occasions that brought them together. He hoped today would go smoothly and pondered the fact he had seven grandchildren: Alfie, Billy, Evelyn, John, Mary, baby Margaret - not a baby now though - and Bill's son, James. A new generation. Let's hope life goes easy on them, he thought as he walked on.

Chapter 11

Sarah rose extra early on Christmas morning to pluck and prepare the pheasant and vegetables. She decided not to disturb sleeping Alfie, who would be back in work the next day, and had earned a rest after the demands of the Christmas season at Coopers. She slipped a pinafore over her long grey dress, and pinned up her once dark curls - now greying at the temples - then peeked into the children's room to find them sleeping soundly, before descending the stairs, taking care not to tread on the creaky steps.

Once safely in the kitchen, she was greeted by the gift Alfie left for her the night before. It was beautifully wrapped in the way only Cooper's specialist wrappers knew how. She smiled as she thought of the effort he would have gone to in order to get a girl to wrap the gift for him. It was almost too good to open! She pulled the red ribbon and brown paper wrapping to reveal a black box inside of which lay a beautiful cameo brooch which she pinned to her dress, and felt like a queen as she lifted the pheasant from its hook in the pantry. At eight o'clock, Jane arrived with two chairs and a bag of vegetables sent by Billy and Mary, who would be over after Mass. Jane helped dress the children and tied huge bows in the girls' hair, ready for Alfie to take them along to Saint Oswald's.

Sarah and Jane, raised by their Scottish father, loosely followed his faith and were not obliged to attend the Mass, but Alfie made sure the children went because he knew Father Mac would count heads.

Sarah saw them off from the doorstep, full of pride, as she watched them hand in hand with their father and Uncle Bill and Auntie Mary. Ma Haggerty was in situ and waved across at her.

'Would yer not consider going yerself, Sarah, lass?' she called.

'Now then, Ma! Don't start that! We all make our own way to Heaven.' Sarah responded, hands on hips. 'Will you have a bit of dinner with us today?'

'That's kind of you, thanks, but Father Mac's calling in with a plate of something fer me. He's a great man, so he is!'

'He is, Ma. I'll be over later with a mince pie or two,' Sarah promised, and went inside to join Jane at the kitchen table with a cup of tea. Relieved at last to have her sister to herself and hopefully hear the news of Callum.

'He can't remember me,' Jane said, her face pale and immobile.

Sarah smiled, 'Can't remember you? Of course he can. Who could forget you? He's havin' you on!' She tried not to let her impatience show. Whatever was going on with Callum? He seemed such a lovely man. Who would have thought he'd mess Jane around in this way?

'No, really, Sarah. He can't remember anything. He's shell-shocked and his memory has gone. They couldn't do anything for him in the hospital in Paris, so he was sent to Alder Hey hospital. He's with his mother now, but will go to a home for veterans after Christmas.'

'There must be something they can do?' Sarah sipped her tea, trying to remain calm and positive for her sister's sake.

'I went to his house, Sarah. Spoke to his mother. Saw him.'

A silence filled with sadness followed. There was nothing much to be said. It was as if she hadn't lost him as she feared, but in reality, he was lost to her.

'The doctors say we must wait and hope.'

A loud knock at the door disturbed the moment, and Jane placed a finger on her lips.

'Not a word to anyone, please, Sarah. It's Christmas Day. We must be jolly.' She banished the sadness from her eyes and opened the door to Granddad John.

'The blessings of the season to you both,' John smiled, as Jane took his hand to help him up the steps.

'It's a long walk from town for an old man. Do you have a drop of beer, Sarah, me luv?'

Jane took his coat and he lowered himself into Alfie's armchair while Sarah poured him a tankard of beer from the jug she had ready.

Within an hour, the chaos of the day was underway, with thirteen people jostling for space in the little house. Jane and Sarah barely had any time to think about their secrets, although Sarah had to take a break in the front room after serving the Christmas pudding, feeling faint for a while.

'She's been up since the crack of dawn,' Alf senior remarked when Auntie Mary drew his attention to Sarah's absence. 'Must be havin' a rest.'

'Well then, I'll lend a hand with the washing up,' Auntie Mary offered. 'It's been lovely today, and that meal was out of this world!'

'Good lass, Mary love,' said Uncle Bill. 'Let's get this place tidied up and us men can go outside for a pipe and beer.

Everyone pitched in to help with the clean-up, including little Maggie, who brought plates to the scullery for Auntie Mary to wash and Auntie Jane to dry. At two o'clock, the men took chairs outside to enjoy a beer while the children also escaped the confines of the house to play on the street with their new toys. Skipping ropes, spinning tops, marbles, jacks and footballs emerged from the houses with excited children, and Ulster Road buzzed with festive cheer as the winter sun shone through a thin layer of cloud.

Granddad John and his two sons put the past behind them for a while and enjoyed the lively atmosphere, while Jane, Sarah and Mary strolled up the road to Ma Haggerty's with mince pies. Alfie, Billy and John played football on the field and Eva entertained her little sisters with the skipping rope Santa had packed in her stocking. It was a perfect day; the sort of day that lingers in the memory as a reference point when trying to recall good times after life has been marred by tragedy.

Granddad John caught the last tram back to town and as darkness fell and the chill crept in, the residents of Ulster Road retreated to the warmth of their stoves. Only when they were alone and tucked up in bed, did Sarah find the moment to break the news of the baby to Alfie.

'We're blessed with our family, don't you think, Alf?'

'We are indeed, my lovely.' Alfie agreed.

'Maggie's growing fast. Not a baby anymore.'

'She's a gem of a girl. Did you see her helping with the table clearing? She doesn't like to be left out.' Alfie smiled at the image of little Maggie carrying an enormous plate with great care and handing it to her auntie Mary, proud of her achievement.

They fell silent as an owl hooted somewhere in a distant wood and shadows cast by a flickering street light, danced on the ceiling.

'What would you say if I told you we have another baby on the way?'

The owl stopped hooting as if listening for an answer.

Chapter 12

Alfie mentioned no misgivings he may have had regarding an extra mouth to feed. The prospect of new life in the family was greeted with excitement, and although the winter was long and harsh, the impact was softened by the thought that summer would bring not only warmth but a baby brother or sister. Maggie's bundle of outgrown outfits was resurrected and laundered. New knitting projects kept Sarah, Jane and Auntie Mary busy whenever they found a moment; blankets, matinee coats, mittens and booties grew from their needles, providing plenty of reasons to get together and compare results, as well as a good opportunity for Eva and young Mary to practice their skills. It was slow going for Mary, but Eva's white blanket proved a success for her as she frequently measured it against her arm.

'It's up to my elbow now, Mammy,'

'Keep going, Eve. The baby will thank you for it one day,' Sarah would encourage. 'Mary's is a holy blanket. Father Mac will be pleased with that one,' she laughed as Mary's small fingers clung tight to the needles while she tried to keep the stitches on.

'Don't worry, Mary. The baby will be happy with your blanket, too.'

The old wooden cradle, used by all the children in infancy, was polished and placed beside the bed in Mammy and Daddy's room, invoking memories of each of the new-born arrivals.

'Who'd have thought we'd one day be living in Old Swan expectin' baby number seven when young Alf came along, and him now a handsome fella with a job on the docks and a girlfriend? Said Sarah as she covered the cot with a sheet to keep the dust away.

Young Alf's new girlfriend was a supposition rather than a fact as yet. It had recently been noted that Alf was taking more than the usual interest in his appearance, and spending more time out and about. However, as much as Sarah was keen to meet her, she was wise enough to avoid direct questions, and patient enough to wait for her son to introduce the young lady when the time was right. But now and then, she would attempt a mild inquisition.

'I see you've bought new shirts, Alf. Not like you to splash out on clothes. I'd have patched your old ones if I'd known they needed mending.'

'So, I bought new shirts, Mam. What's odd about that? Lads need shirts, you know, an' the old ones are fine, just old.'

'But two new ones in a week is unusual. Is there a special occasion?'

'No, Mam. Just wanted a couple of shirts!'

'That's nice and if there was a special reason, you'd tell me, wouldn't you?' Sarah winked, but Alf was not forthcoming.

'Well, whoever the girl is, I hope she doesn't lead him up the garden path and break his heart.' Sarah mused as she and Alfie senior lay in bed that night.

'Sarah, me darlin', I think you're letting your imagination run away with you. He only bought a couple of new shirts, it doesn't necessarily follow that he has a girlfriend, so stop fretting.'

Hard though it was, Sarah put the notion to one side, only for it to be replaced by another of her worries.

'How do you think Jane's coping?'

'With what?' Alfie resigned himself to the fact that Sarah had things on her mind as usual, and sleep may have to wait.

'With Cal's situation. It's such a tragic thing, Alf, for him to be home but not himself. They were so close, and then that bloody war happened. I don't think she'll ever get over him. She sees him every week at the nursing home, hoping he'll have a breakthrough and remember her. It's so hard.' She wiped away a tear.

Alfie tried not to think about the 'bloody' war. He tried but often failed to block the memories, and was thankful to have returned in one piece and be able to support his wife and children.

'I wish there was something to be done, and who knows? He might snap out of it one day.'

'Do you really think he might?'

'We have to believe it's possible, love. Now try to get some sleep.' He kissed her forehead and turned to the window, hoping to drift off himself, but the war was on his mind and it would be a while before he banished the images that haunted him whenever the memories were triggered.

Chapter 13

Jane visited Callum in January at a nursing home tucked away along a leafy lane beyond Knotty Ash. The journey involved a tram ride, then a half-hour walk, and the nurses were very welcoming when she arrived chilled to the bone from icy winter blasts. It was a Georgian house with pleasant rooms filled with natural light pouring through large multi-paned windows. Generous coal fires burned in marble fireplaces and chandeliers hung from the ceiling. Callum would sit beside the fire in a cosy armchair, smoking his pipe and gazing at the flames. Jane would sit opposite, and they would pass the time of day, but he had no recollection of their past together. She was just another visitor, as was the case with his parents and siblings and friends, all of whom felt the pain and grief of having lost the man they knew but were grateful for his presence.

'It's a sorrow I must bear,' she told Sarah as they knitted by the stove one evening. 'I'll never marry now, and will visit Callum for as long as I'm able.'

'That bloody, bloody war!'

Winter dragged its heels through the long plod to spring. Alfie rode back and forth on the tram to Coopers, often despairing at the sight of ragged children on the cold streets as the tram trundled through the city. He sometimes recalled his own childhood when passing Great Newton Street where he was born, and Brownlow Hill Workhouse where he and his siblings spent two years of their childhood. The place was still standing, and it pained him to think about the inmates and the despair they must feel but, as with the war memories, he stored the workhouse away. One day he may explode with the strain of containing his past, but for now he had his family and the routine of work to keep the thoughts at bay.

He would arrive at Coopers at eight o'clock each morning and climb the stairs to his office where his desk overlooked busy Church Street, offering many distractions.

Where once horse-drawn carriages ruled the road, cars jostled for space, while men in suits and women with the new bobbed hairstyle, cloche hats and low-waisted coats browsed the shops. On Church Street, wealthy folk migrating to the United States shopped for goods to take with them on the journey.

Alfie's sign-writing skills were in constant demand, providing him with a useful extra income. Besides some work from shops in Old Swan, and the unpaid work he did for Father Mac, he now and then wrote tickets for his old workhouse friend Russian Alex, who owned a second-hand clothes stall in the market.

'Here, Alfie, my friend. Take this bundle to Sarah,' Alex said one freezing February lunchtime when Alfie arrived with a new batch of tickets for the stall.

'Clothes for the kids, good ones. Came from a rich family leaving for America. God help them.' He blew hot steamy breath on his fingers to warm them.

'Why God help them?' Alfie asked, examining the contents of the bundle.

'America! Too far. Why they want to go there? We have everything in Liverpool! Makes no sense.'

'New opportunities, Alex. New start for their families. I can see the point, but it's not for me an' Sarah. We're happy where we are.'

'Me too, Alfie. Got my Sophie and the stall. And you! Coopers! You made the big time.' They laughed together, 'I remember you in handwriting lessons with that brutal workhouse teacher, always caning me, but you were the expert, my friend.'

Alfie frowned at the memory. 'We've moved on, Alex,' he said. 'We survived it.'

Later that day, Sarah and Jane opened the bundle and were delighted to find jumpers and socks for the boys, together with stockings and two warm coats for Eva and Mary.

'Good old Alex,' Sarah smiled. 'These jumpers will do for Billy and John. They're good quality and John's elbows are wearing thin on the hand-me-downs he got from Bill.'

Jane agreed and carried the clothes to the back room for laundering.

'I'll take the darning needle to the old ones,' she said resolutely. The girls were delighted with their new clothes when they emerged from the laundering room, and Mary was curious to know more about their former owners.

'They've gone to America,' Sarah informed her.

'What's America?' asked a Mary, stroking her new green coat as if it were a kitten.

'It's a place a long way off; three weeks on a boat,' Sarah answered patiently.

'Three weeks! Mam, that's a long time and I think the little girl will miss her coat but I'm happy Alex thought of us.'

'That little girl will be too busy sailing to think about her coat, Mary love, and if she knew you had it, she'd be happy with that.'

March arrived with rain and gales, but the weather grew a little milder and slowly life became easier as the longer days crept in, and here and there a crocus or daffodil pushed through the sodden soil.

'Not long now, Sarah,' Ma Haggerty called across the road one day as Sarah arrived home from the shops laden with two baskets of food. 'You shouldn't be carryin' that lot in your condition, queen.'

'Hello, Ma! I'll drop the shopping off and pop across with a couple of hot cross buns I made this mornin',' Sarah replied and within five minutes she was seated beside Ma Haggerty, enjoying the fruits of her labours. Hot cross buns were her speciality in the run up to Easter Sunday, and very popular with the neighbours. She noticed Ma was thinner and less robust than usual. The winter had taken its toll.

'How are you, Ma?' she asked, concerned. 'You don't look too good. Have you been poorly?'

'I'll be honest with you, it's been an 'ard few weeks, but I think I'm over the worst so thought I'd sit in the warm sun for a while. Not that it's all that warm, mind., but there is a bit of somethin' to bring out the daffodils.' She indicated the meadow a few feet to her right where the bright yellow flowers stood triumphant, having braved the cold to be early bloomers.

'Don't you love it when spring arrives?' said Sarah. So good to know we made it through another winter.'

'Yes, I'm partial to the spring, so I am. The flowers and cherry blossom back home were lovely, and on Easter Sunday we had the vigil and wore white on the day, with our best hats. Our Mam was so proud of us ...' she trailed off and fell into a nostalgic reverie, hardly aware of Sarah's presence.

The two sat in silence a while, sipping their tea until Ma Haggerty's voice rose from her soul and she rendered the most haunting of songs Sarah ever heard; bringing the neighbours out to their doorsteps and those who could, wandered along to where she sat on her rickety chair on the corner of Ulster Road, channelling the fields and crofts of Mayo before the famine. How it used to be when her family went to Easter Mass. The song drifted across the meadow and Sarah sensed it was a special song and that it was possible Ma was getting ready to go home.

Chapter 14

Not long after, Sarah drew back the curtains early one morning and glanced out the window to see Father Mac hurrying along the road with his black bag. She rushed to the front door and opened it to get a better look at where he was heading and, as she suspected, he entered Ma Haggerty's house where a small gathering of neighbours stood, arms folded, talking quietly. She put the door on the latch and crossed the road to join them.

'She's on 'er way out,' Kathleen Finney, Ma's next-door neighbour whispered when Sarah arrived. 'Woke me up with knockin' on the wall an' I 'ave a spare key, so went in.' She stopped to compose herself, visibly upset. Sarah waited to hear the details, her heart pounding. She didn't want Ulster Road to be without Ma Haggerty.

'Found 'er on the floor in a pool of blood,' Kathleen went on. She's 'ad a fall by the looks of it. So our Paddy ran for Father Mac and Lizzie went to fetch the doctor.' The priest emerged from the house and addressed the gathering.

'Our good friend and diamond of Old Swan, Deidre Haggerty has sadly passed away.'

Silence fell and after a moment Father Mac blessed them all, then, too upset to say more, he went on his way.

The funeral was a grand affair with four horses pulling the black carriage, and an abundance of daffodils to decorate the coffin.

Over two hundred people followed Deidre Haggerty to the cemetery in a long, silent procession through Old Swan and up Saint Oswald's Street. The requiem Latin Mass was a beautiful affair, and the choir sang like angels and, as the coffin reached the grave, Ma's neighbours sang one of her songs and it seemed strange to be without her to lead them.

They welcomed baby Francis the summer of 1921, a year of heat, draught and high unemployment around the county. Men marched from Liverpool to Westminster to protest about the cost of living and lack of opportunity in the job market. Young Alfie joined the line of men waiting for dock work every day hoping to be chosen, but the line grew longer and sometimes he was unlucky.

'Thing is, Mam, they all need work and some have families to feed, so I 'ave to be thankful for what I get,' he explained as Sarah tried to cheer him up with a generous bowl of piping hot scouse and a thick slice of freshly baked bread.

'The whole country's the same, love. We'll have to ride the storm as best we can. At least your dad's secure in his work. There's not so many people able to write tickets as good as him. Mightn't be the best paid job in the land, but it's steady in an unsteady world.'

Billy arrived home from his after school delivery round, rosy cheeked from cycling in the sunshine.

'Billy, lad! There y'are. What's been happening with you today? Anything new?'

Sarah ladled a bowl of scouse and placed it on the table, hoping to hear some cheerful news for a change.

'Not a lot, Mam. Still waitin' to hear about the buildin' apprenticeship, an' lookin' forward to the last ever school day.'

'Seems only yesterday you started school,' Sarah sighed.

Eva, Maggie and John tumbled in through the back door, excited after a race home, and Sarah sliced more bread and set out four bowls ready for the scouse.

'Where's our Mary?' Eva asked as she helped Maggie sit on the chair, which was too high for the little one to reach.

'Mary? She should be with you. Didn't you wait for her?' Sarah replied, rubbing the dirt from John's hands with a wet cloth. 'Have you been rollin' around in the muck again, Johny, boy?'

'Just a game of footy, Mam. I scored two goals at lunchtime.'

'Helen said she saw Mary walk away and thought she was coming home,' Eva answered, puzzled by Mary's unusual behaviour. Her brother and sisters always waited at the school gate for her. There was a brief silence while the family considered seven year-old Mary's absence, and Alf noticed an anxious frown cross his mother's face.

'I'll walk up to the school. She's probably waiting there for you, Eve.' He said, pulling his boots on.

'Thanks, Alfie, I can't leave these,' said Sarah. Indicating the children. 'She'll be waitin'. She's a good girl and wouldn't walk off.' Closing the door on Alf, she busied herself with baby Frankie.

Mary, finding herself without a sibling at the school gate as the boisterous children filed out, decided to walk her friend Anne to the corner of Saint Oswald's Street to continue their chat, but walked further than intended, and when she finally set off back to school, took a wrong turn and strayed into a stampede of workers leaving their factory. A man took her by the hand and led her out of the throng, but once away from the confusion, he held on and, to Mary's dismay, pulled her along in the direction she knew to be wrong. No matter how hard she twisted and pulled her hand away, he would not let go.

Alfie walked the familiar route to school and searched the school grounds to no avail, then returned to Ulster Road, confident that little Mary would be home by now, but Sarah's face when he arrived without her induced panic. It was unlike any of the children to wander off. They were a tight-knit family and knew the rules. Eva's heart was racing, and she could not hold back the tears.

'Where's Mary, Mammy?' she pleaded, hoping Sarah would provide a comforting answer, but no comfort came.

'Go out until you find her, Alfie,' Sarah demanded, and Alfie obeyed. He loved all his siblings, but Mary had a special place in his heart. Born the day before his birthday in 1914, her arrival was a beautiful distraction from the war that threatened to change their world. He must find her before dark.

Turning right from the front door, he hurried to the end of the street and on to Prescot Road, where the shopkeepers were putting their shutters up.

'Alfie, lad! Where are you rushing off to?' Mr Pegram called across the road. 'You're in a mighty hurry!' Alf crossed the tram line to where Mr Pegram waited to greet him. 'What's wrong, lad? You look as if you've lost a shillin' and found a penny,' he laughed.

'Mr Pegram, have you seen our Mary? Little, fair hair,' he gestured to show her height.

'I know Mary and yes, she walked past here about ten minutes ago with a fella holding her hand.'

Alfie's heart skipped a beat. 'She didn't come home from school. We don't know that man,' he explained hastily. 'I have to find them.' Alfie turned to leave, but Mr Pegram took his arm.

'Take the bike, Alf,' he said, easing the delivery bike from the doorway. Alfie jumped on and sped away towards Queen's Drive.

Alf senior saw his son dodging the cars and carts from the tram window and wondered what he was up to.

Early evening darkness was creeping in when he arrived at the house to find his family silent around the table. Within seconds of hearing the news, he ran from the house and along the street, then in the direction he saw Alfie cycling. 'Dear God, let Mary be unharmed,' he pleaded as he ran. A huddle of shopkeepers and late shoppers had gathered outside Pegrams, as Mr Pegram spread the news that a little girl had been taken, and asked if anyone else saw her with a man.

'That way, Alf!' Mr Pegram bellowed across the road when he caught sight of the distressed father. A few young lads joined the chase and were soon away up the road ahead of struggling Alfie. He saw them stop and wave to something ahead, then young Alf appeared on the bike with Mary in the basket. There was an audible sigh of relief.

'Daddy!' Mary cried, a tear-stained face revealing her distress as her father pulled her from the basket and held her close.

'Good lad, Alf,' he said, patting his son on the back. Young Alfie was pale with anger. 'He got away, Dad,' he spoke through his teeth.

'Don't worry about that now, son. She's safe. That's all that matters. The police can do the rest.'

Mary received hugs, kisses, and scoldings from Sarah and Eva when she arrived home, while young Alfie was the hero.

Chapter 15

Mary's abduction became embedded in the family folklore and no child left the house without stark warnings of how to react if approached by a stranger.

'One thing's for sure, Sarah. It's not likely to happen again and she wasn't harmed,' Jane poured tea for her sister as they took ten minutes for a sit down and catch up. Soon the schools would finish for their summer break and life would get hectic with the children at home all day.

'They won't be wanderin' off anywhere this summer, Jane. They can play out in the street or on the field, but our Eva will have to keep an eye on the littluns,' Sarah sighed worriedly. And Jane wondered if she would ever recover from the shock of Mary's brief disappearance.

'Here, drink y'tea while it's hot,' she said, handing Sarah a cup and saucer. 'When's Maude coming, by the way?' she asked in an attempt to haul Sarah out of her anxious state.

'In the morning on the ten o'clock tram, according to Alf. It'll be nice to see her after so long, though I'm not sure why she's suddenly decided to visit. It'll be her first time at Ulster Road, so I'm trying to spruce the place up a bit. I'll pop to the shops for a bunch of flowers later. Are you going to call in to say hello?'

'I will if I get a minute. I'm mad busy with Holy Communion dresses an' shirts. All the hand-me-downs need freshening up and it seems half of Old Swan have a child goin' for the big day!'

'As long as our Mary's is ready, that's what matters,' Sarah laughed, nudging Jane with her elbow as she gathered the dishes to wash and they both returned to the business of the day, albeit reluctantly in the sweltering heat.

Cousin Maude lived with her husband and children on Smithdown Road. She was Alf senior's cousin and was very close to his sister, Catherine. The two girls had been the same age and were like sisters despite their different physical appearance. Maud had a mass of dark ringlets while Catherine, pale and slight with lank fair hair, resembled her niece, Mary. Catherine's death broke Maude's heart, and she found it hard to rise from the despair, but time healed, and life moved on. A new generation of the family emerged, to whom Catherine's name meant nothing.

Sarah, with baby Frankie on her hip, met the ten o'clock tram as it arrived on time, as always. Maude emerged, her mass of dark, now greying hair pinned up off her face and wearing a pale blue cotton dress.

'Sarah, love!' Maude gushed, embracing both mother and child. 'How lovely to see you after so long, and the baby is adorable! A lot like his father. So, this is Old Swan? Can't imagine why it took me so long to come here. Life, I suppose. We're always too busy for the things that matter most. Here, let me carry baby.

'Frankie,' Sarah said, handing a disgruntled Frankie to Maude and wondering, not for the first time why Maude had come. The last occasion they met was at Catherine's funeral, although she kept in touch with Alf off and on. Working in town, as he did, he was more prone to chance meetings with old friends and family, whereas Old Swan required a bit of an effort to reach.

'Welcome, Maude! Follow me; we have to cross the road, then it's a short walk to our house.' Sarah led the way until they reached Ulster Road, lined on either side with smart terraced houses, cheerful in the heat.

'How pretty,' said Maude, 'More colourful than I imagined, and handy little shops. I expected something duller.' Sarah could not disguise her puzzlement at this remark.

'Duller? In truth, Maude, there's never a dull moment here in Old Swan; not in our house, anyway. That's Billy and Mary's house across the road. Jane lives with them and takes in washing. This is our place.' Sarah fumbled in her apron pocket for her key and opened the door. It was cool inside, and Sarah left her visitor to settle in the front room while she went to the kitchen to pour glasses of home-made lemonade.

'This'll refresh you after the hot tram ride,' she said, handing Maude her drink. She lifted Frankie from the floor where Maude had placed him as he wriggled free from her grasp and, sinking into the chair opposite her guest, proceeded to feed him.

'I love your little house, Sarah. So homely and cosy - you have a great gift for home-making, I must say.' Maude's admiring eyes scanned the room. 'It can't be easy keeping a place clean and tidy with such a lot of children running around,' she smiled.

'It's not so bad, Maude. I have them all trained and Eva's a great help.' She placed the now sleeping Frankie on the couch.

'Well, I won't beat about the bush, Sarah, love. It's Eva I'm here about. I met Alf in town the other day and he mentioned Eva will be leaving school next year and she may be looking for work.' A horse and cart rattled by outside and Sarah's heart skipped a beat at the thought of her Eva going out to work and being away from her. She was not ready to consider the possibility, and resented the fact that Alfie had discussed it with Maude. She may be his cousin, but hardly close enough to play a role in their first daughter's future.

'I suppose she may be thinkin' along those lines, but truth is, we haven't talked much about it and I'm not sure I could manage without her at home.'

'Yes, I know what you mean. I felt the same about my Florrie when the time came. It's not easy to let them go ...' a pause ensued; a wistful moment shared by the two to acknowledge how ruthless time could be.

'So, anyway,' Maude continued, 'I wanted to let you know there's a position coming up in a house in Sefton Park. They're looking for a live-in maid to start next May. It's a good household close to where I worked when I was Eva's age.' Maude realised from the look of shock on Sarah's face that she was delivering unwelcome news.

'Living in?' Sarah's world fell apart at the thought.

'Yes, it's quite normal and will free up a bit of space in your house,' Maude decided to point out the practicalities.

'We manage the space very well, thank you and not for one moment have I ever had the idea that Eva would move out. I don't think she'd want to anyway.' Sarah picked up the glasses and returned to the kitchen. 'Would you like another drink?' she asked, remembering her manners.

'No, but thank you, Sarah, I have to catch the midday tram and want to see a bit of Old Swan while I'm here, but now I know where you live I hope we can do this again, perhaps when Alfie and Billy can be here. We have a lot of catching up to do. There's plenty of time for you and Eva to think about the offer. I know the girl who's leaving, and she's very happy in the house, which is one of the reasons I thought of Eva. Good employers are hard to find.' Maude rose to leave.

'It was kind of you to think about us and I promise we'll give it some thought. I'm just not sure we could ever do without our Eve.'

Maude left Sarah on the doorstep and made her way along Ulster Road. Sarah waited until she turned the corner and shuddered as she thought about the changes ahead. Then, glancing across to Ma Haggerty's house, she could have sworn the old woman was sitting there on her old chair, watching.

Chapter 16

'You should've warned me she was coming to talk about our Eva leavin' home, Alf. It took me by surprise, and I wasn't very nice. The thought's never crossed my mind.'

Alfie and Sarah were in bed at the end of another long hot day and, as was usually the case, Sarah snatched the chance to confide in her husband at the only time they had any privacy together.

'I thought you'd be happy with the idea. Eva will have to find something for when she leaves school and if Maude recommends a place, I'm sure we can trust her.' Alf pushed the blanket away in an effort to cool down.

'Yes, Alf, she'll have to find something but not living in. I'd miss her too much. It's a *no*, and that's that!'

There was no further response from Alfie and Sarah assumed he had drifted off to sleep, but in truth, he decided this was not a discussion he wanted to have right now, and feigning sleep would be the best way to go.

'And after Maude left, I saw Ma Haggerty sat outside her house; just like she always used to. Starin' down the road at me. Gave me the creeps, Alf. Why would she do that?' Alfie remained silent and only a distant owl responded as she lay fathoming the disturbing nature of the day's events.

Eva reacted indifferently to the question of her future. Next year was a long way away, and she was enjoying the present too much to care, although she felt a strange delight at the possibility of having a break from her siblings, but it was a fleeting thought. Her days were busy. She never had a minute to herself. She liked school, but only so she could be with her friends. She had never been a great scholar but could read, write and do her sums well enough to get by. Life beyond never occurred to her. Who would take Mary and Maggie to school and bring them home? Who would help Mam with the shopping and baking? Mary wasn't old enough yet, and she was too much of a dreamer to be responsible for Maggie. These thoughts filled her head whenever she dwelt on the future, so she avoided them.

Helen was her best friend and together they would chat about clothes, hairstyles, film stars and boys. On the long summer evenings, the young people of Ulster Road would gather beneath the lamppost on the corner near the meadow. Some of the boys would kick a football through the wild poppy strewn grass while the girls played hopscotch or, if a skipping rope turned up with one of them, they would take turns holding ends while the rest lined up for their turn running under or jumping over. Now and then a grown up joined in and the neighbours sitting outside enjoying the cool evening would cheer them on until they gave up, winded by the effort.

'I don't know where the kids find the energy!' they would gasp, re-joining their peers to much hilarity.

When the younger children went inside, older boys and girls stayed out to flirt and dream and carve their names on the end wall bricks until darkness fell.

'Don't make noise!' Sarah would say as Alfie, Billy, Eva and John drifted in, having enjoyed the final dregs of the night with their mates. 'I've just got Frankie to sleep!'

Chapter 17

The summer of 1922 would remain in the Cattell's collective memories as the jewel of summers. Billy left school and joined young Alf in the building trade, and the two would set off early morning for a day of labouring on one of the many buildings going up in the city. Billy's ambition, since seeing the ornate ceiling at the game-keeper's cottage, was to become a plasterer.

John was artistic like his father and grandfather, and Alfie senior began to teach him his trade.

'If you're good enough by the time you leave school, John, I'll arrange for you to have an apprenticeship at Coopers with me, but you'll have to work at it and be patient.'

Whenever they asked about his childhood, he would tell them he went to a boarding school in Brownlow Hill. A white lie that avoided the need to revisit the trauma of his early years.

Working with his father appealed to John, and he imagined himself in a smart suit taking the tram to town and being part of the 'Cooper crew,' as his dad called them, and he would spend some time improving his handwriting skills and completing tasks set for him by his father. However, he was a restless boy and after an hour he would be ready to release the stored energy out on the meadow with his friends and a football. His real dream was to be a footballer and play for Everton or Liverpool, and for that he needed practise, so every day throughout the summer he and his mates would take jam butties and flasks of water to the field - returning home only to replenish food and drink supplies.

'There you are, stranger!' Sarah would joke whenever he burst in through the back door; nut brown with sun burn that made his green eyes greener and his fair hair fairer. 'My handsome lad!' she would smile as she sliced and buttered the bread for him. 'You'll break a few hearts when you grow up!'

'Thanks, Mam! See you at teatime,' John would call as he ran out the front door.

'Go out the back door!' Sarah would shout after him, but it would always be too late; he would be up the road and on the field, before she could reach the door and close it after him.

Maggie and Mary spent a lot of time walking Frankie up and down the road, each holding a hand and patiently waiting when he wanted to stop and inspect something or say hello to a neighbour.

'And who might this be?' the elderly neighbours would ask.

'Tell 'im y'name, Frankie,' Maggie would instruct her little brother.

'Panky,' he would reply with an enchanting smile.

'Panky, is it? The neighbour would repeat, and they would all have a laugh. 'Well, Panky, here's a sweety, and one each for y'sisters,' Mary and Maggie would look surprised and take the sweets with much gratitude.

Eva stayed indoors helping her mam, and would sometimes go across the road to her uncle Bill's and help Jane with the washing, before calling on Helen early evening to catch up on the day's events.

And so passed the time of that precious summer, when all was well and the sun shone every day. September crept in with a flurry of clothes mending and shoe fixing. If they fit a pair of feet, they would re-sole and heel them, if not they would pass them on to a needy family. This kept the new shoe buying to a minimum. They moved Maggie into Mary's dresses, Mary into Eva's, and John into Billy's shirts and trousers. The school routine resumed as darkness encroached and autumn leaves began to fall.

The day school resumed brought great relief for Sarah who set about scrubbing the floor, polishing furniture and scouring the stove, while Frankie, wondering why his sisters had deserted him, played with wooden building blocks and went shopping along Old Swan in his pram with his mam.

'Frankie'll soon be too big f'that pram,' Sarah announced to Alfie one night when the children slept and the house was quiet. She handed him a cup of warm, sweet milk with a dram of whisky to prepare him for the news she was about to impart. Alfie placed the drink on the chair arm and settled back with his pipe to study the flames of the fire dancing in the hearth. It was their time to reflect on the day and share a few anecdotes about life in the upper-crust Coopers store, and life at the helm of their family ship; steering through calm waters or rough. Sarah would giggle at Alfie's tales of the rich young things about town in their dashing outfits, while Sarah made light of the mundane affairs of the day. This night, however, she was waiting for the right moment and wondering how she could prepare him.

'He's growing into a fine lad,' Alf puffed at his pipe. 'He could walk beside the pram and you can stack the shopping in it,' he said, offering the sort of advice only those with no experience of shopping with small children offer. 'We'll soon have done with that pram.' Sarah found her moment.

'Or we might need it for a little longer,' she ventured.

'Well, I can't see Frankie being in it much beyond October but it's up to you, your territory,' he pulled a tobacco tin from his pocket, removed a few strands to fill the bowl of his old mahogany pipe, struck a match and held the bright flame over the bowl taking deep puffs until it glowed, then raised his eyes to meet Sarah's unamused gaze.

'Our children are our territory, Alfie Cattell! I'm trying to tell you something if only you'd stop playing with that pipe of yours and pay attention.'

Alfie looked stung and let out a cloud of aromatic smoke. 'Go on then tell me and stop beatin' about the bush!'

'I'm pregnant,' she said.

Alf drew another mouthful of smoke and exhaled. His face showed no discernible reaction.

'In that case, Sally, you're right. We'd better not throw the pram out and someone'll have to budge up in bed to make room for another one.' Their eyes met, and they held the gaze for a full minute; a minute in which all the fears, anguish and joy the prospect of another little being in their home entailed were spoken without a word passing their lips.

Chapter 18

Winter dug in and the people of Liverpool braced themselves for the inevitable rain, wind, snow, and dark. Knitting needles were unearthed, and bundles of wool turned into scarves, gloves, cardigans, jumpers and blankets. Doorstep chats were replaced by stove-side knitting sessions, the front line of defence against the weather which brought colds, flu, bronchitis, pneumonia and many other ailments to take their toll on the poor, the elderly and the frail. When the knitting was done for the family, they would knit for charity, and at school the girls had knitting classes - some struggled to keep stitches on needles long enough to make a square to become part of a patchwork quilt for a person in need.

Sarah sent the children to school with bellies full of porridge.

'That'll keep y'going until y'next meal,' she would say, placing a steaming bowl on the table for each of her brood, and sure enough they all glowed with good health as they waved goodbye to their mammy and Frankie, and made their way along the alley to school.

There would never be another winter like it for them. The familiar pattern of days unfolded; the same contented rhythm of life with its ups and downs rooted in a solid foundation of family love. The young ones racing to school and home with tales of their day, and the older ones out at work and home with tales of their day. So many tales to hear, dreams forming and, in young Alfie's case, romance budding.

'It's that girl from Montague Road,' Jane announced. 'The one with flaming red hair. Geraldine,' I saw them together when I went to drop the washin' off at the Smiths.'

There had been speculation regarding young Alf and his recent attention to grooming his hair and spending his earnings on smart clothes. He was a strong, good-looking young man with dark, rugged looks and bright blue eyes.

'Is that so?' Sarah responded, rolling the pastry she was preparing for the chicken pie with a little more vigour. 'She'll have to be something special to deserve our Alfie.'

Jane chuckled to herself as she dutifully agreed with her sister. She'll have to let them go one day, she thought. Can't hold on to them for life.

That day came too soon. It was a Saturday in December when Sara's thoughts were occupied by the cold weather, the shopping, the baby in her womb, the Christmas pudding making, Alfie's girlfriend, and all the little things that busied her thoughts on December Saturdays - hardly a thought or a glance or a word was cast to the one she was about to lose. It was a normal day.

'I need to run to the shops for ten minutes to pick up the fruit for the pudding. You lot stay inside. Eva, keep an eye on them, I won't be long,' she called and closed the door.

Later, she would replay those moments, so carefree, with no backward glance. Just going out for ten minutes. Had she left five minutes later it wouldn't have happened. Had she picked up the fruit the day before, it wouldn't have happened. Had the football been burst or lost, it wouldn't have happened, or had the tractor taken another route, broken down, been a little slower, it wouldn't have happened.

But it did.

John picked up the football, ignored his sister's cries: 'Mam said we've to stay in the house!'

Ran out the front door and into the road where the tractor driver had no chance to brake. In a moment too horrific to contemplate, John lost his life, and everything changed.

Ulster Road fell quiet for days as the Cattells grieved their loss. Father Mac came to console and pray with the distraught family. John's coffin was carried on a horse-drawn cart to his resting place on the sixteenth of December. A sad procession of family and young friends dazed by the sudden loss of a bright life.

Sarah would blame herself, Eva would blame herself, but blame was inconceivable. It was a trick of fate, a synchronicity of chance that led to John's death on that cruel grey day.

Jane and Auntie Mary, together with a band of kind neighbours, took over the running of the house, while Alf Senior and Sarah dealt with their grief. They cooked meals, cared for bewildered children, and cleaned the house. Meanwhile, Father Mac would visit to reassure them that John was at peace with the angels.

'Are you sure about that, Father?' Sarah would ask, and Father Mac, whose giant presence filled the room, promised it was true.

'If I'm wrong, Sarah dear, I'll eat my hat,' he said, and Sarah took comfort from the thought.

After a while, the needs of the family drew them back from their despair, and they attended to their wounded children. In time, they began to talk about John.

'Remember when he lost a shoe in the meadow and took all morning searching for it?'

'And the day he ate all the cake Mam made for Ma Haggerty?'

'And when he climbed over Mr Jim's wall and was chased by his mad dog'

They began to laugh again, and it was a relief after weeks of sadness.

'He hasn't left us,' Sarah told them. 'Father Mac says he's an angel now, and that's what I want us all to remember. Our John hasn't left us and we must never lock the back door in case he needs to come in.'

Meanwhile, Alf Senior returned to work in grief and not a day would pass without him riding the tram tormented by thoughts of John and his plans to serve his apprenticeship at Coopers, how they would have travelled to work together, and how he would have watched his talent grow ... and then he would smile a faint smile and recall John's restless spirit and how in truth he wanted to be a footballer, until the sadness returned and he would quickly wipe away a tear. Such a waste of a bright life. His son no more.

The daily tram commute, being as it was, a regular journey to work for most of the passengers, they got to know one another and were familiar with who got on and where, who got off and where. Hence, Alfie's travelling friends missed him and, upon hearing the sad news, expressed sympathy, offered condolences, and sat in silence with him on the day of his return. At work, his colleagues greeted him with the same thoughtful consideration until the demands of the day eventually drew his mind away from the harrowing thoughts.

Chapter 19

'Well now, Sarah,' said Father Mac, seated on the couch in the lounge. His big presence warmed the room.

He took the tea from Sarah and waited for her to settle in the armchair beside the stove. They sipped the hot drink. The clock ticked and sounds of the street - neighbours passing the time of day, a horse and cart shambling by and a lone dog barking in a backyard - penetrated the thickness of the silence. The children were at school and Frankie was across the road at Billy and Mary's house, while Father Mac had 'a few words' with Sarah.

'What's he coming here for?' Sarah had snapped when Alfie told her the priest planned to visit that day. 'I'm not one of his flock, Alf. Much as I like the man, I don't know why he needs to visit me.' She pulled a bright red jumper over Frankie's head and pushed his arms into the sleeves then planted a kiss on his cool forehead.

'I'm not sure why, love. Well, could be he needs to have a word about a cake he wants baking,' Alfie replied, avoiding any serious avenues of speculation, although he knew the reason, having spoken to the good man after Mass on Sunday. Father Mac had taken him to one side as he filed out of the church into the frosty morning sun, and enquired about the family.

'How're you all bearing up, Alf?' he asked.

'Learning to live with our loss, Father Mac,' Alf replied. 'It's been hard, you know. And I worry about my Sarah, at home all day thinking and waiting for John to come running in like he used to. It's hard on us all, but Sarah's not out in the world with the distractions, you know, Father? She's there all the time in her old routine, but without John,' he pulled his cap on and turned to leave.

'I'll call and see her in the morning!' Father Mac had said and Alfie left, wondering if he'd said too much. Sarah could be somewhat rebellious when it came to his church, although she had a soft spot for Father Mac.

'A cake? Why would he want me to bake him a cake, Alf? He has a housekeeper, doesn't he? It can't be about a cake!' Sarah was clattering pots and pans in the kitchen, annoyed her routine was about to be disturbed by a priest, of all things.

'Tara, love. See y'later!' Alf called and gently closing the front door, set off for work at speed before one of the pans was flung in his direction.

'So, well now, Sarah. How are you doin'? I'll come right out with it and tell you your Alf is concerned that you're havin' a wee bit of trouble pullin' y'self out of the grief.' The kind priest paused to gauge Sara's reaction and saw that she was listening, but expressionless. He ventured on.

'It's natural. In fact, you'll always have it, the grief. It stays.'

Sarah's calm brown eyes met his. 'I know,' she said softly, and the two shared another silence.

'I hear you've a talent for the cake making,' said Father Mac after a while, and Sarah smiled faintly.

'Well now, we're having a bit of a gatherin' for a few of the parish old folk and I was wondering if you'd have the time to do a bit of bakin' for it. I'll provide the ingredients, of course.

'How many are you thinking?' asked Sarah.

'To be sure, it depends on the size, but I was thinking five or six large and fifty of the tiddlers, you know, cupcakes.'

Sarah's eyes widened. 'When for?'

'A week today,' said Father Mac, sensing hope in the air.

I'll do it,' Sarah agreed.

'Grand! Send your Eva with a list of whatever's needed, and she can pick it up next day.' He heaved himself up from the couch and made his way to the door.

'I'll do that, Father,' said Sarah.

'It's a deal! See you next week with the cakes.'

He stepped into the busy street and breathed in the crisp February air. Satisfied with the outcome, he hurried back to the priest's house where he would have to plan the old folk's event which, until ten minutes ago, had not existed.

'Take a shopping list where?' Eva quizzed on hearing Sarah's unexpected request.

'To Father Mac at the priest's house, Eva,' Sarah replied. 'You heard the first time. He asked me to bake cakes for the old folks gatherin', but he needs a list of ingredients. It's a big order else I'd get it meself. Will you do that for me, please?'

'Course I will, Mam. Me an' Helen will take it after tea.'

On the way to the priest's house, as they ambled along towards Saint Oswald's Street, Eva read the list. 'I think Mam's making cakes for an army, Helly. Don't know how she'll get them made in time for the do.'

'Her arm will drop off with all that mixing,' Helen observed, reading the list over Eva's shoulder.

The two wore black bucket hats decorated with sprigs of red berries with smart drop waisted coats and linked arms as they went.

'It's the first time I've seen any life in Mam's eyes since … you know,' said Eva.

'Since John passed, you mean?' Helen came to her aid.

'Yes,' Eva replied, her voice faint.

'Sounds like it'll do her good to make the cakes. I'll bring a mixin' bowl over and lend a hand if it helps.'

'Thanks, Helly, I'll let her know.' Eva was moved by the offer and secretly felt a spark of excitement - something she never thought she could feel again.

'Well now, girls,' Father Mac beamed as they stood before him in the polished office of the priest's house. 'I take it you've brought the list for the cakes?'

'Yes, Father,' Eva replied, shyly handing it across the table.

Father Mac glanced at the paper and Sarah's neat handwriting.

'That's a lot of eggs!' he smiled. 'Tell your Mammy I'll have it delivered tomorrow, and we'll need the cakes for the tea party on Monday afternoon, so if she can get them to us by eleven that day, that will be dandy.' He winked at the girls.

'I'll let her know, Father,' Eva replied, and the two hastened to the door, eager to leave the formality of the room.

'All that polish makes me feel sick,' Helen remarked once they were clear of the church. 'Imagine living with that all your life!'

'I like Father Mac, though. He's a kind man,' said Eva, suspecting a little conjuring on his part. If Father Mac's plan had been to help heal her mother, he couldn't have chosen a better way.

Chapter 20

Sarah gathered her team that Saturday to lay out her plan. The cake ingredients were delivered, checked, and stored in the pantry. Sarah assigned tasks to Jane, Eva, and Helen for the next day's baking, and they located and lined up all the equipment for an early start.

'Preparation is the key to success,' Sarah informed them. 'Those were the very words Sadie Smith used to repeat over and over. I can hear her now,' Sarah smiled at the memory of her old boss at the baker's shop. 'That's where I met your dad, Eva. He came in with Billy and Colleen one day, lookin' for battenberg for Colleen's dad. Sadie asked me to bring an apple pie from the kitchen, and there I was icin' a weddin' cake, so I had to break off what I was doin' to find the pie and take it through to the shop. I remember the first sight of your dad, just a young lad an' shy as anythin', blue eyes, blushin' you know, but handsome. I gave him the pie and went back to the weddin' cake. After that he was never away from the shop, then one day he asked me out, an' that was that. Never a day's regret.' Sarah eyed her transfixed audience, unused to such nostalgic moments. 'So, anyway, Sadie would always tell me "preparation is key!"'

'Mammy, that's a lovely story. You've never told us that one,' Eva fibbed, having heard it several times, but she never tired of it. 'Who's Colleen?' she asked, pleased to see some of the old spark return to her mother.

'Colleen was a friend of your auntie Catherine who died young. God rest her soul. She was from Ireland and had a sister called Bernadette. She an' your uncle Billy were very close, but the girls went back to Ireland and Billy went to sea, and in the end it didn't work out for them Then Billy met your auntie Mary an' they fell in love,'

Sarah returned to the practicalities of preparing for the big baking day and her helpers followed suit.

That Sunday was a day they would talk about for many years to come. Sarah and Jane worked on the three-layered Victoria sponge cakes while Helen and Eva concentrated on the cupcakes. Chatter and laughter filled the house. Delighted by the lively turn of events, Mary, Maggie and Frankie stood on chairs and helped with weighing and mixing, until Frankie tried to smash an egg on the table and the girls reluctantly took him for a walk. Young Alfie and Billy hung around hoping to bag a spare cup-cake, with the promise to transport the finished products safely to the priest's house.

When the neighbours got wind of what was happening at the Cattell's house, some called in to see if they could help in any way, then went home to bake a few cakes for the old people. Alf Senior, who had joked to Sarah that perhaps Father Mac wanted a word about a cake, couldn't believe the turn of events. It was like they had their old Sarah back, and not only that, but the children were laughing again.

Our John would've loved this,' Sarah remarked, busily creaming sugar into butter and cracking eggs on the side of her earthenware mixing bowl. The gathering paused for a moment's silent reflection before agreeing and getting on with the job.

Three ovens were used to bake the cakes: Sara's, Helen's mother's and Auntie Mary's, and by the end of the day the results of their labours stood proudly on Sarah's kitchen table; three Victoria sponge sandwich cakes layered with strawberry jam and cream then topped with a dusting of icing sugar and fifty-five cup-cakes iced in white and pink and blue.

'Mrs Beeton would be proud of us,' said Sarah, admiring their work.

'She would if she were alive,' Jane laughed.

'Y'can't beat her recipes! Sadie Smith swore by them,' Sarah pronounced.

Once they were placed in good sized tins, the boys - having enjoyed a cup-cake or two - delivered them to a grateful Father Mac ready for the feast.

After washing the pots and clearing the kitchen of a dusting of flour and icing sugar that had settled in every crevice, the bakers rested in the front room. Sarah put her feet up on a stool and rubbed her swollen ankles.

'You need to take it easy now, love,' said Alf Senior, laying a tray of tea down for the workers. 'You've the baby to think of.'

'Dad's right, Mam,' Eva nodded, pouring tea into the Sunday best China cups and handing them round.' Not long now before my new sister or brother arrives.'

'Matter of weeks,' Jane agreed. 'I'd better get knitting!'

'Well, there's a bundle of wool tucked away in the sideboard and we need to fish out Frankie's cast offs,'

'And the cradle,' Alfie mused. 'I'll smarten it up with a lick of paint.'

Chapter 21

James Cattell arrived in April with the tulips and daffodils.

New life.

Frankie moved into the big bedroom with his brothers and sisters while James slept in the cradle beside Sarah.

'Mammy, I've been thinking about what cousin Maude said,' Eva ventured when she returned from school one shower strewn day in May.

Sarah thrust a crying baby James into Eva's arms and turned to Frankie who had a splinter in his finger from playing in the backyard.

'Hold still, Frank,' she tweezed the splinter out and wiped his finger with antiseptic. Tears dried and finger better, Frankie ran to play again and Sarah, controlling the heartbreak, turned to Eva.

'Why would you want that, love? You won't be happy away from us all. I know you won't. You're too much of a home bird an' think how much Mary and Maggie will miss you, not to mention Frank an' the baby! And me!' Sarah took the now soothed James from Eva and awaited her response. Her world would crash if Eva left, and so soon after John. How would she cope? But her countenance remained stern, revealing nothing of the pain inside.

'Yes, Mam, I know. I've thought a lot about all of that, and I know I'll miss all of you, but Mary and Maggie will help out with Frank and James. I just think It's a good chance for me to learn something and earn money to help out here. Maude said the family is good, an' I'll have to do somethin' when I leave school.'

'There's plenty for you to do round here. Eva,'

'I need to earn my keep, Mam.' Eva looked pleadingly at her mother. It hadn't been an easy decision. She had many conversations with Helen about taking the job or staying home, but the truth was that after John's death, she struggled in silence with the guilt she felt. Her mother told her to look after the children and she failed. Now there was another child to look after and she did not feel up to it anymore. The job in Sefton Park would take her away from the responsibilities and give her some time to herself. Sharing a bed with Mary and Maggie was getting harder. She was becoming a woman and needed privacy. Her mind was made up.

'We'll talk to your dad about it later,' Sarah concluded. 'Set the table for tea, please.' Eva knew by her tone that Sarah was strongly against her going, and from experience she knew how hard it was to persuade her mother when her mind was made up.

Once the family had eaten, the younger children asleep, and Billy and Alfie were out, Alf senior settled down with his pipe and a copy of the *Liverpool Echo*, to catch up on the news, but peace was not forthcoming.

'Our Eva wants to leave home an' go to work for that posh family in Sefton Park, Alf. It's all the fault of that meddlin' cousin of yours, Maude. I could wring her neck! What right has she to come here an' interfere with our family? Puttin' ideas into my daughter's head! I'm not allowin' it an' that's that!' She handed Alf a cup of tea and settled into her chair to face him.

Alf took the tea and balanced it on the arm of his chair, considering his response. He had a lot of empathy for Eva's situation. His own life had taught him how important it is to make your own way in the world. The workhouse regime was tough, but he emerged with a skill which, with help from his father, set him up for life. His sister Catherine was a milliner and dressmaker, his beloved Sarah, a confectioner. It was important for Eva to get started with her own future, and staying home to help her mother would only hinder that. He puffed on his pipe, feeling the glare of Sarah's angry eyes. Finally, he met her gaze.

'I say, let her go,' he ventured. 'Life moves on, love. It's time for Eva to steer her own road. Who's to know? She may be home within a week, but at least she'll have had a go.'

Sarah was silent. She knew her husband well and had prepared herself for his response. Throughout the day, her thoughts had battled with arguments and counterarguments regarding Eva's leaving home, and she had steeled herself for

Alf's measured and sensible decision - which was as she had expected - and, weary of the turmoil, she would respect it.

'So be it,' she sighed, resigned to change, and at the top of the stairs, where she sat listening, Eva wiped tears of gratitude from her eyes.

Plans and preparations for Eva's leaving home became the priority focus for the family. Alf senior had a word with Maude who arranged for her to visit her new employer, a brief interview with Mrs Manning, the house-keeper, established that Eva would begin work in June when the present maid, Stella would have left, and she could be 'taught the ropes,' as Mrs Manning put it.

Eva chattered away to her mother about the splendour of the house: 'I only made it to the kitchen to meet Mrs Manning, but what a kitchen, Mam! Pots an' pans as big as our Frankie! You could fit ten of our house into that one.' Frankie perched on her lap happily playing with a toy, unaware his beloved Eva would soon be gone.

Sarah listened with feigned interest. She struggled to be enthusiastic about the turn of events, but tried for her daughter's sake. Eva, meanwhile, was aware of her mother's feelings, and did her best to ease the way for her departure.

'Mary, you'll have to help Mam a lot when I go. I'll show you how to wash dishes an' peel spuds,' Eva whispered as they lay in bed one warm summer night.

'What if we don't want you to go?' Mary enquired, daunted at the prospect of filling Eva's capable shoes.

'It's not a choice, Mary! I have to go. Mrs Manning's expecting me.'

'Who's she when she's at home?' Mary asked.

'Mrs Manning is the House-keeper and my boss,' Eva replied.

'So she'll be bossin' you around, same way you boss us?' Mary asked, surprised.

'Well, not exactly the same way, Mary! Now go to sleep!'

Mary obeyed as Eva considered the prospect of being bossed around, not something she was used to, but hopefully, Mrs Manning would be a kind boss.

The day Eva left school - a few weeks early to take up employment - Alfie junior finally brought his girlfriend home, ending the speculation regarding his improved appearance and staying out late. But apart from the sighting reported by Jane, no real confirmation of a steady relationship until the balmy stock-scented evening in June when Geraldine was ushered into the house through the back door - in order to avoid gossipy neighbours.

Sarah and the girls were clearing the table and doing the washing up - each with their own responsibility in the process; with Maggie carrying the small items from the table, Mary, the plates and cups, Eva washing the dishes and Sarah drying and putting away. The routine was well established and efficient, although not necessarily ideal, as Eva often pointed out.

'Mam, it's time the boys helped a bit,' Eva would complain.

'They get away with too much and the suffragettes say we women 'ave to fight back.'

'That's all very well, young lady, but the dishes don't do themselves, an' the day one of my lads does them will be the day the sun freezes over. I can't wait that long,' Sarah would say.

'Anyway, it's good practice for your new job. Take it from me, you'll be sick of washing dishes after a week!' Sarah laughed, and Eva rolled her eyes, unamused.

'Mammy, this is Geraldine,' Alfie interrupted, and the busy scene became a tableau, frozen in time, while Geraldine came under scrutiny and blushed.

'Hello,' she ventured and took Alfie's hand.

Sarah's thoughts went spinning into the future, and she conjured an image of Geraldine and Alfie at the altar, getting married.

She would lose another precious child.

'Geraldine?' she said, hoping the poor girl would not detect the resentment she felt from her tone. Then, noticing her son's anguish, remembered her manners. 'Come an' sit down, Geraldine. I'll put these pots away an' come an' join you. Alfie, get Geraldine a drink of lemonade from the pantry.'

Sarah and the girls finished off the washing up and all settled around the table to watch the Geraldine show. Mary thought she was beautiful; like the Lady of Shallot from a poem she learned at school. She had a pure white face and long red hair. 'Are you our Alfie's girlfriend?' she asked and Geraldine blushed again.

'Yes she is, Mary.' Alfie answered, looking directly at Sarah as if challenging her to object. It had taken a while for him to find the courage to bring his girl home, and now that he had, he was desperate for her to be accepted. As he placed a glass of lemonade on the table for Geraldine, baby James awoke crying. Sarah hurried to the front room and returned with James in her arms. Geraldine, forgetting her shyness, rose from her seat and joined Sarah at the top of the table.

'A baby! Alfie, you didn't tell be you had a baby in the family!' She peered at the red-faced James with his mop of dark hair and brown eyes. 'Can I hold him, Mrs Cattell?' she pleaded.

'It's hard to keep up,' said Alfie. 'Last time I looked, Frankie was the baby. Now we've got Baby Bunting,' he laughed.

Sarah transferred the crying bundle from her arms to Geraldine's.

'Baby Bunting?' Geraldine smiled. 'Is that what you call him?'

'We call him Bunty,' said Maggie, standing beside Geraldine's chair and patting Bunty on the head.

'Gently, now, Mags,' Sarah cautioned.

'I'm being gentle, Mam,' Maggie reassured.

At that moment, Alf senior arrived home and fended off the stampede of children running to greet him.

'Alf's got a Geraldine!' Maggie informed him.

'A Geraldine?'

'Yes, she looks like the Lady of Shallot!' said Mary.

'Well, Mary, I think that lady's dead, so let's hope she doesn't really look like her.'

'She looks like the picture at school,' Mary giggled.

When curious Alfie reached the kitchen and looked to see this paragon of beauty, his heart melted at the sight of the skinny young girl whose red hair was so long she could sit on it. In her arms, she held the baby, who contentedly gurgled as he studied the unfamiliar face.

'This is Geraldine, Daddy,' said Alf junior.

'Welcome, Geraldine!' said Alfie. 'Mary's right, you know, you're the double of the Lady of Shallot,' he laughed. 'The absolute double!'

Chapter 22

Geraldine's arrival stirred a confusion of emotions within the family. Sarah had to admit she took a liking to her straight away, but the thought of losing her son, Alfie to another woman, a perfectly natural occurrence, made her afraid. She could not bear the thought. It was too soon. She needed to keep her children around her, but Eva was going, and her Alfie had a girl.

'It's the way of things, Sarah, love,' said Jane, gently counselling her sister as they drank tea at the kitchen table the day after Geraldin's arrival.

'It's a good thing for your Alfie to have a girl and from what I've heard of her, she's a good one. Works at Sturla's in the petticoats, I believe. She might get us some discount.'

Jane sipped her tea and studied Sarah's bewildered face, etched with grief and fear of further loss. Sarah met her gaze and smiled.

'Petticoats? Is that what she does?' A ponderous silence ensued.

'In that case, Jane, I might come to like her.' Sarah said, with a wink.

'A woman can never have enough of them!' said Jane with a broad grin, and the sisters descended into fits of laughter.

Meanwhile, Eva, on the brink of leaving home, also had mixed feelings about Geraldine's arrival. Perhaps she would be around to help Sarah out - an extra pair of hands now and then. This would be a good thing and would lessen the guilt she felt about leaving her mother to cope with the children and housework. On the other hand, she felt jealous of the girl her father made such a fuss of, and who Mary called beautiful. She imagined Geraldine would replace her in the family while she slaved away in a stranger's house. The children would love

Geraldine and forget about her. She thought about giving up on the job.

'That would be a daft thing to do, Evie,' Helen advised when her friend confided her fears.

'It might sound daft to you, Helly, but I'm the one who walked them to school and home. I'm the one who helped feed them and pushed them around Old Swan in the pram until they slept. Not that Geraldine with her beautiful hair!' Eva was ready to explode with anger.

'Evie! The poor girl only called to say hello, and she's Alfie's girlfriend, so you'd better get used to her. She might be your sister-in-law one day.'

'I know that much. I'm only mad because I'm goin' away and she'll be there while I'm not,' said Eva.

'Give it time. See how it works out.' Helen soothed. 'What'll I do without you?'

The two linked arms and strolled the streets of Old Swan that summer evening, conscious everything was about to change, and the familiar routines that had governed their lives would soon dissolve and become pleasant memories.

On the Sunday before Eva left home to start employment, Sarah made a roast dinner and bought a large Victoria sponge cake. Geraldine joined them for the meal, winning Eva over with the gift of a white cotton petticoat to wear under her work dress.

'What colour dress will you be wearing at the big house?' Maggie enquired.

'Black in the morning and blue in the afternoon to serve the meal,' Eva replied.

'Two dresses in one day!'

'Yes, they don't want the maid to serve the meal in dirty clothes an' in the mornings I'll be cleanin' out the fireplaces an' scrubbing pots an' pans.' Eva informed them. Maggie burst into tears, and Mary put a comforting arm round her shoulders.

'It's alright Maggie, she'll come home sometimes,' said Mary.

'She'll be home every Sunday, Mags, and we'll have a special meal to celebrate,' said Sarah, who felt much as Maggie did but managed to hold back the tears. Later that day, Eva packed her bag, ready for the early morning tram.

Chapter 23

April Manning watched Eva from the kitchen window as she walked timidly up the path of the house in Sefton Park. The slender young girl carried an old leather suitcase and wore a green cotton sleeveless dress with a stylish low waist and a yellow cloche hat. Her dark hair was curled at the shoulders and her pale face betrayed the fear she felt.

As April watched, she recalled that feeling: leaving home for the first time, entering a strange house and putting your trust in people you have never met. Her experience had not been a good one, but times had changed and whenever a new employee arrived at the house, she tried to help them settle in. Little Eva wouldn't find it easy, but once she started working, she would have no time to dwell on her former life.

Opening the door, she greeted the new maid with a smile and ushered her into the kitchen.

'Welcome, Evelyn. Come inside and take a seat while I put the kettle on for a cup of tea. It's a hot day for tram travel.'

Eva sat at the sturdy scrubbed pine table and placed her suitcase on the stone tiled floor. She felt her face burn red with embarrassment. How could she ever be a part of this grand house, this vast kitchen where everything was ten times bigger than in their little house on Ulster Road?

'After tea and a nice slice of cake, I'll take you up to your room.'

Eva mustered a faint smile and sipped her tea, wondering how she would tell Mrs Manning she could not stay.

'Then I'll run you through your duties and y'might as well make a start,' April concluded, knowing full well that Eva would be planning an escape. A knock at the door distracted her, and she opened it to a delivery man with a tray of buns.

'Come in, Jack, and put 'em on the table here.'

'Right you are, Mrs Manning,' said young Jack as he placed the tray as instructed.

'This is Evelyn, our new maid. Starts today so she may take in the orders now an' then. Here, Evelyn, when Jack comes, be sure to check the order before you sign for it. This one's for ten buns, so I'll count the buns and sign Jack's book, then Jack will give me the receipt.' April demonstrated the procedure and Eva nodded to show she understood.

'I'll be off then,' said Jack. 'See you in the mornin'!'

April saw him out, then turned to Eva. 'Let's get you up to your room, Evelyn. There's a day's work to do, an' you'll need to get ready for it. I'll fit you with a dress from the laundry room on the way.'

Together, they climbed the narrow stairwell, stopping midway to find the blue and black dresses and white aprons.

'You'll be visiting this room often, Evelyn. Here are the sheets and pillowcases, tablecloths, napkins ...' said April, deftly pointing to each pile. 'But we'll come back later for a longer look around.'

Eva stood in awe of the shelves piled high with linen ware and thought about her auntie Jane, working long hours to launder a fraction of the contents of this room.

'Let's get on now.' April ushered Eva out of the room and up two more flights of stairs. The final stairwell narrower than the others - more like a ship's ladder with flimsy steps leading to a small, draughty attic. 'It's not much, but you have your own bed. This one's yours,' she said, indicating a narrow, board like structure covered with a grey blanket. There's a wardrobe for you to hang your clothes in. I'll leave you to get changed. Come down to the kitchen when you're ready.' Whereupon April left the room and Eva.

Chapter 24

'Do you think Eva's alright, Alf? I'm worried she'll be missing us,'

'She'll be fine, and I'd worry if she wasn't missing us,' said Alf, staring at the bedroom ceiling. It was early morning the day after Eva left to start work in Sefton Park - that time of day before three-month-old James woke up and bawled for his feed, the brief time of peace when the busy couple listened to the dawn chorus and shared their thoughts.

'I can't believe she's not here in her own bed, Alf love.'

'If I know anything about the way those houses are run, she'll be out of bed an' scrubbing floors already.'

'Oh! Don't say that! Surely not, love. Do you think they'll work her that hard? Poor Eva,' Sarah was close to tears.

'I was pulling your leg. Maude wouldn't get her a place in a cruel house,' Alfie soothed. 'There's our James awake. Time to get out of bed. There's work to be done.'

All through the day Sarah's thoughts were with her oldest daughter and the terrible life she must be leading with total strangers. She sensed Eva's fear and unhappiness; how could she feel happy so far away from everyone who loved her and everything familiar? She missed her presence.

'Mary and Maggie! Take James in the pram an' Frankie for a walk to the end of the road an' back. I need some time to clean the kitchen. See if you can get James to sleep.'

The sisters obeyed; Mary pushed the old pram while Frankie held on to the handle with one hand and Maggie's hand with the other. They walked to the corner of Ulster Road to watch the shoppers and the traffic on Prescot road: trams, horses and carts, cars and bicycles navigated the wide road and people queued for bread, meat and vegetables. They would watch for a while, then turn the pram and make their way back along the pavement where neighbours greeted them and peered in to see the baby.

'What's 'is name, they would ask. 'James but we sometimes call 'im Bunty' Mary would reply.

'Bunty?'

'Or Bunt,' Maggie would add, helpfully.

'Bunt? That's an interestin' name to give a child.'

'He's our baby bunting,' Mary would clarify, and the neighbours would laugh and say how sweet the name and how sweet the baby.

By the end of her first full day of work at the house in Sefton Park, Eva was exhausted. She had dusted every surface in ten rooms, swept and mopped the floors, had her first lesson in laying tables for small banquets, peeled two dozen potatoes and served dessert at dinner. At eight o'clock she ate with the kitchen staff, too weary to think about anything but the uninviting bed in the attic.

'Have a good sleep, Evelyn,' said April Manning after supper. 'Be up at five o'clock in the morning. Take clean dresses and aprons from the laundry room on your way up and drop the soiled ones in there tomorrow. Good night.'

'Good night Mrs Manning,' Eva responded with a voice that had lain somewhere within, unused throughout the strange day.

'You'll hear the knock on your door at half past four. Be in the kitchen at five, prompt.'

She hung the clean dresses and aprons in the wardrobe and lay the used ones near the door to remind her she must drop them off, then pulled on her crisp white cotton nightgown, carefully laundered and starched by Jane. The bed was more comfortable than it appeared, and she lay for a while watching the half-moon which shone through a small skylight window in the sloping ceiling. She lay motionless while her weary bones and muscles relaxed, but her brain kept going. So many things had happened since she left Ulster Road, yesterday. The size of the rooms overwhelmed her, the plush carpets, the flock walls lined with gold framed portraits of stern looking ancestors, the size of the pots and pans, plates and dishes. Why did anyone need so much?

She thought about their house on Ulster Road where she shared a bed with her sisters, and they squashed around the kitchen table and on the old leather suite in the living room. There was never any extra space, but it was enough. She thought about her mammy who would have struggled without her that day, and Mary who would do her best to help, but she was such a dreamer. She thought about her daddy, taking the tram day in, day out, and working hard to keep the family in clothes and fed, and never mentioning the war or complaining about his hard childhood. Then Alfie and Billy with girlfriends now. She hadn't mentioned Billy's girlfriend to Mammy but had seen him with Jean a few times. She smiled at the thought of Billy with a girlfriend. She thought about Maggie with her big brown eyes, who did her best to help and was devoted to Frankie and the baby.

When she had exhausted all other avenues of thought, her mind wandered to the place she avoided; the thoughts she blocked out. The thoughts of John and the years they had together in their home where his presence lingered in every hour of every day, and she tried to block it out. She tried to ignore the spaces he should fill at the table, in the meadow where his friends played football, on the journey to school and home. John would never be there again, and she felt the grip of the grief she had suppressed. Finally, alone in that strange bed beneath the bright moon, she let it go. Her body shook with the sobs that seemed to have lodged in her gut. Now, alone at last, she released them and cried for her brother, John.

Chapter 25

Sarah tossed and turned in her bed that night.

'She'll be home on Sunday, an' she's only at Sefton Park, not America! Get some sleep,' Alfie pleaded. He needed his sleep.

'I'm trying, but just can't manage it tonight. It'll get better, Alf. Once I'm used to her not being around.'

Alfie fell silent, and they both thought about the other child who was not around - he knew John's absence was the reason Sarah could not let Eva go.

An hour passed and Alfie slept, but Sarah's fretful thoughts kept her awake. Was Eva sleeping? Had she eaten? Were they cruel to her? She would fetch her in the morning. Bring her home. With this resolve, her turbulent mind, like the passing of a storm, calmed. She would bring her home, she thought, and sleep drew closer, then from a distant horizon drifted a song. She held her breath to listen harder. It was a thin thread of sound, far away but there nevertheless, and Sarah thought she recognised the melancholy, soulful voice of Ma Haggerty as she drifted off to sleep.

She was wakened by James's cries, and wearily lifting him from the cot, held him close and rocked him until the crying stopped then descended the stairs and placed him on a rag rug near the stove, while she revived the glowing embers with kindling and coal, then filled the kettle and placed it on the hob before she warmed milk for James, washed him with warm water and made him comfortable with fresh clothes then settled down to feed him, cradling him in her arms while he hungrily drank the milk.

In the stillness of that moment, she recalled Ma Haggerty's song. Did she imagine it? Did she dream it? Whatever happened, it brought her peace, and perhaps it was the old woman's way of telling her she was taking care of John. Sarah smiled to herself. Ma always had a soft spot for John.

'He's a handsome lad,' she would say. 'Always laughin' an' kickin' that football.' She glanced up at the ceiling in the direction of Heaven and mouthed the words, 'Thank you, Ma.'

With James settled in the wooden cradle beside the stove, she made a pot of tea and poured herself a cup. Late summer sunlight filtered through the heavy lace curtains and brightened a jam jar filled with buttercups and daisies Mary and Maggie collected from the meadow yesterday. Sarah admired them, although they drooped already. She sipped her tea and glanced beyond the flowers to the space beneath the stairs, where she noticed the familiar old brown leather suitcase. The one her mother carried out of Ireland when she sailed to Liverpool, that and the feather mattress bundled in oilcloth and tied with string; an image that had remained with Sarah since the day her mother told her the story and now she owned the suitcase and the mattress. She wondered why the case was there and not in its usual home on top of the wardrobe in her bedroom. Slowly, the morning fog lifted from her sleep deprived brain until the image of Eva leaving the house with the case emerged. But how had it returned? Did Alfie collect it? She rose from the chair and, puzzled, made her way to the case and picked it up to find it was full. She placed it on the table and opened the brass latches.

'I hated it, Mam.'

Sarah jumped with fright on hearing the words, then turned to see her daughter on the bottom stair, lovely in her white nightdress, soft dark curls licking her shoulders and those azure eyes wide and earnest. Without hesitation, Sarah opened her arms to embrace her child, and Eva ran to her.

'That's alright, love. You gave it a try,' Sarah comforted.

'How did you get home? Let's make tea. We have a while before the others wake. Time for you to tell me all about it.' Eva told her mother how nervous she was when she arrived at the house and how Mrs Manning seemed kind but firm.

'She called me Evelyn, Mam! I wondered who she was talkin' to, then realised it was me.'

Sarah laughed at this. 'It is your name!' she said.

Eva told how the place was far too big for the few people living there, although they had a gathering for dinner.

'It was silver service an' I got it all wrong, and the bed was like a plank, Mam. I didn't sleep a wink an' all I could think about was you an' Daddy, our Bunty an' Frankie an' Mary an' Maggie an' Billy an' Alf an' then John an' I cried an' cried.'

Sarah thought about her own nights without Eva at home.

'So, I had a knock on the door to wake me at four o'clock this morning, packed my bag and walked out. Kept on walking until I got home. Came in through the back door an' went to bed just before Bunty woke up.'

'Well, I was never keen on you going and I couldn't be happier to have you back, Eva, love,' said Sarah, before planting a kiss on Eva's forehead.

As the family emerged from their night's sleep, Eva was greeted with varying degrees of surprise and delight.

'After the restless night your mam had worried about you, Eva, I'm happy to see you home, but we'll have to explain to Mrs Manning and cousin Maude,' said Alf senior.

'That's true, dad but I never want to set foot in that house again,' said Eva, lifting Frankie up and settling him happily on her knee. He was pleased to see his sister.

'Did you miss me, Frankie boy?' she asked, cuddling the sturdy child.

'Miss you? You've hardly been away,' Billy jibed, as he ran down the stairs. 'Why are you home? Did they sack you already?' He was rushing to catch the tram to town and pulled his boots on as he spoke.

'Don't be cheeky! I came home because I couldn't bear to be without you, our Bill,' Eva smiled.

'Oh, indeed! That makes sense, our Eva,' Billy winked. 'I'm away now, tara!' he called and slammed the door behind him.

'That door'll fly off its hinges one of these days, the way you lot treat it!' Sarah lamented, feigning anger when in truth her heart was full now her precious Eva was at home where she belonged.

Chapter 26

The balmy summer evenings of August, when the folk of Ulster Road chatted on doorsteps and children played until late, gave way to foggy autumn and the return to school for Mary and Maggie, smartly dressed in black dresses, white pinafores, black stockings and polished black shoes. Sarah braided their hair and watched them set off on the first day, recalling all the years she had stood at the door watching as her children left for school, their images stamped on her memory. Mary and Maggie would soon be joined by Frankie in another year or so, then Bunty would tag along.

Meanwhile, Eva and Helen were starting work at the Automatic Telephone Company. They had set off together early that morning, the height of fashion, linking arms as they walked to the tram and gossiping like they had been apart for a year.

She hardly saw young Alf or Billy these days; always out at the Regent picture house or dancing with their girls or playing football with their pals.

Where had the years gone since their move to Ulster Road? A new start where the air was clean. Then the war came when Mary was born and Alf's call up just as Maggie was born, then Jane stepping up to help with the children when she was worried enough about her Callum. Alfie and Billy on the delivery bike, then the return of her Alf from the war. Ma Haggerty on the corner and John ...

'Cup of tea, Sarah?' Jane asked. 'I'll drop this bundle of washing in the house, then come over to yours for ten minutes.'

'Right! I'll put the kettle on,' said Sarah.

Jane arrived with two scones she had made that morning, and Sarah brought the tea into the front room where they could relax in comfort while Frankie and Bunty played on the rug.

'Alf's talking about us moving,' said Sarah.

'Moving? Why would you move?' Jane asked, so shocked she spilt her tea.

'He says we need more room, which we do; can't argue with that.'

Sarah sighed.

'Where would you move to?'

'Blackhorse Lane. Alf says he's found a house, number 40, three bedrooms and gardens front and back so we can raise chickens, grow spuds and keep a dog.' Sarah needed her sister's approval, after all they had been through over the years on Ulster Road, they had forged strong bonds. But Alf was right, it was time to move on.

'Sounds perfect!' said Jane, smiling broadly. 'Absolutely perfect!'

END

Printed in Great Britain
by Amazon